DEAD SHIFT

GRAVE TALKER SERIES BOOK FOUR

ANNIE ANDERSON

DEAD SHIFT

ARCANE SOULS WORLD
Grave Talker Book 4

International Bestselling Author
Annie Anderson

Edited by Angela Sanders
Cover Design by Tattered Quill Designs

www.annieande.com

BOOKS BY ANNIE ANDERSON

THE ARCANE SOULS WORLD

GRAVE TALKER SERIES

Dead to Me

Dead & Gone

Dead Calm

Dead Shift

Dead Ahead

SOUL READER SERIES

Night Watch

Death Watch

Grave Watch

THE WRONG WITCH SERIES

Spells & Slip-ups

THE ETHEREAL WORLD

ROGUE ETHEREAL SERIES

Woman of Blood & Bone

Daughter of Souls & Silence

Lady of Madness & Moonlight

Sister of Embers & Echoes

Priestess of Storms & Stone

Queen of Fate & Fire

PHOENIX RISING SERIES

(Formerly the Ashes to Ashes Series)

Flame Kissed

Death Kissed

Fate Kissed

Shade Kissed

Sight Kissed

There should be a rule in the universe somewhere that said if someone—*namely, me*—had already dealt with enough shit, then no one could bother said someone for at least twenty-four hours.

Or maybe forty-eight.

A case could be made for seventy-two as well.

But since such a rule did not exist—at least in this universe—I was stuck with my ass on the grass, staring at a bullshit note and wishing I could explode the sender's brain with my mind. Exploding a brain couldn't be too far outside my new scope of abilities. I'd twisted the heads off a group of ghouls' shoulders a few days ago with no more than a flick of my fingers. Making one measly brain go *poof* should be child's play, right?

If only.

Though, with my teeth rattling around in my head from the ground shaking beneath my feet, I figured maybe, just maybe, my new abilities may not be a good thing. I mean, the wind whipping through the church could possibly have been a fluke, but the ground shaking like a goddamn maraca?

Probably not.

Still, I couldn't peel my eyes from that note to save my life, and more? I didn't want to.

Azrael lied to you. Killian isn't where you think he is.
Come find me when you're ready for the truth.
   —Essex

The man who I'd called "Father" my whole life was in the ground right now, his body moldering in his casket, and the man who'd set it all into motion had the nerve to pick at the bloody scab that was my wounded heart.

I reached for that stupid note, ready to set it on fire or crumble it up, or something, anything but let it lie in the grass where my dad had been put to rest. A hard hand knocked my fingers away before they could make contact, startling me right out of my ill-conceived plan. My sister stared at me like I'd grown a whole new head

—and for good reason. A few months ago, she'd gotten a similar letter from our brother, one that would have killed her had she not been utterly and totally dead already.

"Are you okay?" Sloane asked, rolling her eyes at herself as she did so. She'd asked me that same question quite a lot over the last few days, and each time she seemed to curse herself.

I cradled the hand she'd smacked against my chest as I inspected her features—ones that seemed to flicker every couple of seconds from regular Sloane to one so fucking frightening it was a wonder I wasn't running away screaming.

Poker face, don't fail me now.

"Of course I'm not okay." Which was the god's honest truth. I was so far from okay it was stupid—especially since my totally dead, yet somehow living sister, had started resembling *Skeletor* for some reason. "Are *you* okay?"

Yes, I could have rolled my eyes at myself like she had, but honestly, I was just trying not to freak all the way out. Sure, I'd believed her when she'd said she wasn't alive, but I hadn't actually seen it until now. Add that on top of Essex's bullshit, and *well...*

"No," she croaked, a fine tremor of rage making her entire body shake. "No, I'm not okay."

Sloane appeared like she was about half a second away from sniffing out our bastard of a brother and flaying him alive. But before she could act on what I deemed wholeheartedly as righteous vengeance, a pair of giant hands lifted her off her feet. One second, she was flickering like a burning-out lightbulb, and the next, her face was tucked out of sight, hidden from view as her boyfriend hugged her tight to his chest.

Did one call a six-hundred-year-old mage "boyfriend"?

Considering I had one of those, it seemed somewhat ill-fitting. Lover felt icky, and mate seemed too serious. I'd have to find a different moniker that didn't make me want to hurl.

"Your face, love," Bastian murmured against her hair, holding her close when she tried to push away. "Breathe, Sloane. Tell me what happened."

The kindness in his tone set my teeth on edge. Sure, it was for all the wrong reasons, but my anger and fear and complete inability to handle my own shit had me lashing out, anyway.

"Our bastard of a brother is what happened. See for yourself."

Dutifully, I pointed at the rather obsequious note as I cringed at myself for breaking their moment. Instead of looking, he inspected my sister's face, the utter care stamped all over him, making my heart hurt.

Fucking Essex and his bloody notes. I don't care what the damn thing says. She's not going off alone. Not ever again.

I swallowed thickly, not liking that I could read his thoughts, too. It was bad enough I could see every single ghost in this stupid cemetery, but their souls called out to me, their thoughts, their need to move on. And that was on top of all the living that had yet to disperse from the graveside service. It was one thing to assume that the people you saw on a daily basis thought you were a freak. It was quite another to fucking *know*. I could totally do without Bastian's inner monologue of fear, blind devotion, and near nauseating need to kiss my sister rattling around in my skull.

"I will in a moment," he answered, but his mind was a maelstrom of panic—none of which appeared on his face.

Looking away, I tried to find a spot that didn't have a person—living or dead—to stare at. My options were limited, but I settled on glaring at my shoes and wishing they were anything but the sensible pumps I'd decided to wear. The inspection was short-lived, the presence of the whole damn gang pressing in on me like a visceral weight. I hadn't even looked up, but I knew J and Jimmy were holding hands, the events that led up to today strengthening their bond. I wanted to be happy for them, too, but the happiness was drowned out by the guilt that gnawed at my gut every time I thought about what had been done to them because of my presence in their lives. Bishop followed closely behind them, along with Sloane's vampire friend, Thomas.

Ingrid had spoken very highly of Thomas over the years, but seeing the scant glimpses the ironclad ward that protected his mind allowed, I had to wonder how much my small friend actually knew about her mentor. Did she know how much it hurt him to see Sloane and Bastian together? Or that the rejection from his family burned him to his very core? I wondered if she knew his secrets, if she was aware of just how lonely he felt.

Peering up from my shoes, I took stock of the vamp. He was beautiful in a way that unattainable models were. Sharp cheekbones, razor-sharp jaw, damn near pouty lips—everything about him was severe, too pretty, too... something. His face practically screamed "fuck off" while his body seemed coiled, ready to strike at any moment. He had the same odd stillness to him that Mags did—the kind that only the ancient vamps had.

"You know that's a trap, right?" Thomas growled, his face condescending, but his mind was a whole other matter. Thomas' thoughts were on my sister—on protecting her. And what was funny about it all was I doubted she knew.

"No shit." Sloane sneered. "I hadn't thought, what, with my brother's penchant for deadly notes that could *ever* be a possibility. Whatever will I do without your ancient knowledge, Thomas?"

He raised a perturbed eyebrow, but internally he was trying very hard not to laugh.

"Well, if you wouldn't go running into the fray at every available opportunity, then I wouldn't have to say painfully obvious things, now, would I?" he shot back, rolling his eyes like a certified teenager.

I couldn't help it. I snickered.

Sloane narrowed her eyes at me, her skeleton face gone for the moment. "Like you've got room to talk."

It was true I had zero room to give her shit, but it was still funny. Hence why I stuck my tongue out at her. Her gaze fell back to the ground, the silly cardstock catching her focus. Mine followed, the mirth dying in my chest. I wanted to keep it—mainly to get it off the ground and away from prying eyes—but I wanted to burn it, too.

The rustle of a plastic bag startled me out of my destruction plans. J had somehow gotten from the other side of the group and over to me without me noticing, and in his hands was a pair of blue Nitrile gloves and an evidence bag. I swallowed hard, struggling not to lose it at the sheer awesomeness of my best friend.

"Thank you," I croaked, taking the gloves and donning them by rote. How many times had J handed me a pair of those damn blue gloves? How many times had he been right here for me when I needed him?

And how many times had he been hurt because of this life—the one I dragged him into? J was human, fragile, and that fact was no more apparent now than it had been two days ago when he'd been standing right next to my father as he died. Losing Dad had been a blow, but so was the knowledge that it just as easily could have been J. It could have been him in the ground, could have been him I was mourning.

"No problem, D. You know I've always got your back."

And that was the rub, wasn't it? Having my back was going to get him killed.

With another lump-filled swallow, I took the evidence bag from his fingers and the disposable tongs he'd managed to tuck under his arm. *Trust J to always be prepared for a crime scene—even at a funeral.* Once the letter was stowed inside the plastic, J swiped it from my hands —tongs and all—handing it to Jimmy, who performed some kind of glittering gold mojo on it with a wave of his fingers.

"There," Jimmy said on a sigh. "Now, the spell I see crawling all over that note is contained in the plastic." He shook his head. "Amateur. Like we'd touch a note from that asshole."

J threw an arm over my shoulder, tucking me into his chest. "You know everyone is congregating at Killian's house for the reception. What do you say we avoid that mess, glut ourselves on Blanca's tacos, and watch something good on TV? Dave and Mom have it handled. You don't have to go."

I had a feeling this wasn't going to be comfort food and *Practical Magic*. It was most likely going to be strategy and trying to outthink a homicidal maniac with unlimited resources and a grudge.

Yippee.

"Yeah, come on, Adler," Bishop cajoled as he pulled me out of my best friend's embrace, lacing his fingers with mine. "Don't you want some food and Sandra Bullock?" My gaze found Sarina, who definitely told him my favorite movie, the traitor. "I might even make you a margarita."

The gesture made me smile—a little one, for sure—but Bishop acted like I was a paraplegic walking for the first time, his nearly black eyes practically swimming in relief.

"That's my girl."

I nodded, but my gaze still cut to that damned letter. Sandy, margaritas, and tacos weren't going to fix this shit. Not even a little.

As it turned out, there was very little strategy—*or margaritas*—to be had. Instead of plotting and planning, I was on my favorite chair, resting on Bishop's lap with my face tucked into his neck. Most of the available places to sit were taken up by my sister and our collective friends, and other than the ground shaking every couple of minutes, I was calm as could be.

Granted, every time I thought about Essex's note, the lights in my house flickered like they might explode, but that was neither here nor there.

"So, no one is going to say anything about the penchant for earthquakes this house has?" Harper growled, her voice like the crack of a whip on my brain. I mean, sure, she'd been mentally berating me for a while now, but tossing her voice into the mix was only adding insult to injury. For someone so small, she did pack a mental wallop. "Or the fact that this one is so juiced up she might as well power a nuclear reactor? I mean, I'm all for trying to gather oneself and hiding away, but holy shit, girl, you light up like Vegas every twelve minutes, and a single temper tantrum from you is going to break the planet."

I snorted, not bothering to open my eyes. "Tell me how you really feel, Harper. Don't hold back."

"That *was* me sugarcoating it, sweetheart. You don't want to hear everything I have to say."

Opening a lone eye, I half-glared at the empath. "Maybe I do." Maybe if she said it aloud, she'd stop screeching at me with her mind. I opened the other eye and sat up. "Maybe I want to know what you're holding back."

Harper mirrored me, rising from her pillow of Sarina's lap as she tried to stare me down. "You have too much power running through your veins, no outlet, and you're shaking the fucking planet. Not to mention, no one has said a peep about whether or not the souls roiling under your skin are being put to rest, or what's going to happen now that you've essentially blew up two Knoxville factions. Your father died, and that is awful. Truly, I feel for you, but you have too much going on to just sit here and wallow, especially when you're waving a red fucking flag in front of your brother."

Harper stood, but I was trying to process the massive truth bomb she'd just set off in my living room.

"I feel them whispering under your skin, and I know you do, too. Those souls aren't at rest, and they aren't at peace. You're just another prison for them, and Essex Drake just walked up to you like you were a cute little toddler. I have to wonder why he's not terrified of you, and when I think about that too hard, I get scared."

That same thought had been running through my brain since Essex strolled through the cemetery like it was nothing. And one look at Sloane's face confirmed she was thinking the same damn thing I was. "I'm scared, too. But I don't know if I can fix it or even how I'm supposed to. Azrael is MIA again, and… I don't trust myself to go up against Essex. I don't trust myself to walk out in public or say hi to my neighbors or go back to work. I'm just trying to breathe here."

"Why can't we put the souls back in the ring?" my sister asked, an option I'd considered and discarded about a thousand times in the last three hours. "Your body can't hold them without causing seismic activity, right? And you're not absorbing them like normal. Then, why can't we just shove them back in the ring, pawn it off to Azrael, and have his feathery ass deal with it?"

Because he wouldn't come if I called him. Because he doesn't care. Because… he cares too much about upsetting some deluded idea of balance that he'd let me die.

"As if he would even help," I muttered instead, resettling on Bishop's lap. His arms circled me, his fingers sifting through my hair as he massaged my scalp.

"Then he doesn't help. But you can't keep those souls inside you forever," Sloane barked. "Because sooner or later Essex is just going to tap you like a keg and suck them out, and then we're just as fucked as we were two damn days ago."

It would have hurt less if she had slapped me instead. Without a thought, I got to my feet—ready to do what, I had no idea.

"You know they're right, D," J said from his perch on the floor, cuddled up to Jimmy. "You can't keep all that bottled up forever. If it doesn't kill your body, it sure as hell will kill your mind."

Well, he might as well have stabbed me. "You think I don't know that? You think I can't read all your thoughts, feel all your emotions? You think I don't feel your ideas just buzzing in the back of my mind?" I tried and failed to hold my bitter tears inside. "I know I can't do this forever. I can barely handle today."

"Then what do you plan to do about it?" Thomas asked from his place on the couch, a glass of my father's favorite whiskey in his hand. "Because all I see is a scared child who runs the risk of turning out just like the parents she hates so much. If you're the woman I think you are, I would hope the safety of those around you would be your top priority."

I ground my teeth together to keep my rage tamped

down, but still, the house rattled so hard, a crack hissed up my living room wall.

Fuck. Don't kill him. Don't kill him. Don't kill him.

"But I suppose choosing to throw a temper tantrum is more your speed then?"

"Really?" Sloane squawked. "Antagonizing her? This is your plan?"

Thomas jerked his chin to spear her with a bored glare. "It worked on you, didn't it?"

His face was filled with apathy, but his mind was a sea of bottled-up love and a boatload of regret. That and Bishop's warm hand on my back had me unclenching my fists and jaw.

"Okay. I will agree something needs to be done, but I don't trust Azrael, and I don't believe Essex, and I don't know what will happen if I extract these souls. So, if we could figure that out, that would be great. In the meantime, I think everyone should head home."

I needed everyone out. I needed silence and not to feel everything from everyone all the time. I needed a glimpse of peace just so I could think for one fucking minute. But when everyone else stood to leave, Bastian and Darby stayed put.

"I mean you, too. You've stayed here for two days. I don't need a babysitter anymore."

"The hell you don't," Sloane protested. "Essex is still out there—"

"And I've got back up here if he decides to pick a fight. You have a life and a home that doesn't include me. It's about time you went back to it."

J and Jimmy would be next door, so it wasn't like I would be totally alone, anyway.

"This is a horrible plan, you know."

Shrugging, I snorted. "Probably. But at least my house will be empty."

"Fine. But I swear to everything holy, if something happens while I'm gone, and you get killed, I am retrieving you from the Underworld and kicking your ass," she threatened, pointing at me like she was chiding a three-year-old kid.

"Promises, promises," I muttered.

Honestly? I had a feeling there was far more truth to that statement than either of us wanted to admit.

2

After I ushered Sloane and Bastian out of my house, I realized I had another couple of stragglers to deal with. Getting them out of my home was going to require far more spoons than I had. Gathering my mental fortitude, I rested my forehead on my door, wishing everyone would take the damn hint.

"I mean you guys, too," I muttered, but I had a good feeling both of them were listening to me. Neither one had so much as let me out of their sight since... I swallowed, shaking my head to dispel the memory of that stupid fucking knife.

Still, I saw it, anyway—the blade flipping end over end as it sailed through the air. The way it almost thudded as it hit its mark.

"I'll be doin' no such thing, lass," Hildy argued. "You painted a bigger target on your arse than you might realize. I'm not goin' anywhere."

Practically grinding my teeth together, I shot my ghostly grandfather a glare. "Then watch my back from outside. I need a moment of peace before I burn the whole damn world to the ground. So if you don't mind, I need you to leave. Go bug J and Jimmy. Go find some ghouls for me to kill. Go nuts, but *go*."

Hildy pursed his lips, contemplating his options. His mind was a mess of protective ire and more than a little grief. It was a grief he didn't want, but it was still there, nonetheless. As much as I appreciated him being here for me, the fact that he still mourned Mariana burned me up inside. There was only so much of that I could take before I summarily lost it.

"As you wish, lass. But I'm coming back. You can't get rid of me forever."

"Like a bad penny," I muttered with a smile on my face, so he knew I still loved him.

He returned my grin and then winked out of sight.

One down. One to go.

Turning, I finally faced the man that was actually going to be a problem. Bishop stood in my kitchen, his hands braced on my counter as he stared me down.

"No," he growled, a hint of gold coloring his irises.

"I'm not going anywhere, Adler. It's bad enough I had to stand by and let you get hurt. It's bad enough that I couldn't... I couldn't..." He trailed off, shaking his head. "No, babe. I'm not doing it. I'm not leaving you here to wallow in guilt or think up another way to put yourself in danger. Not again."

I tossed up my hands. What did he think I was going to do? Hightail it to Knoxville and start blowing things up? Go on the prowl for witches? Figure out how to hunt down my bastard of a brother and explode his innards?

Okay, so all of those were possibilities, but highly unlikely.

"What if I just wanted silence?"

He chuckled, slowly shaking his head at me. "I was born at night, but it wasn't last night. There's more rage running through you than sense right now."

What was with everyone dropping the most cutting truths today? Jesus. I mean, I knew I was a little off, but didn't I get to be? Didn't I get to hurt and mourn and grieve? Honestly, it took me a second to remember that I loved this man, or else I was going to slap the ever-loving shit out of him.

Nodding, I pursed my lips. In fact, I had to stare at my feet because if I looked at him for one more second, I was going to do something stupid.

"I know you don't want to hear it, and that's fine." His voice had grown considerably closer than it had been before, but I was still mad and refused to look up. "You don't want to talk, that's cool, too. But there is not a single reality where I leave you to grieve alone. Where I nod and smile and fuck off like a good little boy so you can deal with this shit on your own."

A finger found its way under my chin, and then I was staring into once-obsidian eyes that now flashed with the gold of his power. What was it about those eyes that affected me so much differently when he was this close?

"So we can fight," he offered, his voice like gravel, "or we can fuck, or we can cuddle on that goddamn couch, but you aren't getting rid of me. Ever."

Bishop's mind was a swirl of images—with him so near, his thoughts bombarded me with them—the pair of us twisted together, our hot breath mingling as we explored each other. He was dying to taste my skin, practically aching to touch me anywhere, everywhere.

These were thoughts I could get on board with. Without a second's hesitation, I rose up on my toes, nipping his bottom lip as I ran my nose against his.

"I choose option number two."

Bishop's eyes grew heavy-lidded as he prowled closer, his movements causing me to take a few steps back until the door stopped me. The dichotomy had me shivering

—the cool wood against my back and the blistering warmth of Bishop against my front. His fingers found their way into my hair, gently pulling as he tilted up my chin.

I wanted him to kiss me. Hell, I wanted him to rip my clothes off and make me forget everything that had transpired over the last three days. Something, anything. I reached for him—ready to do a little clothes ripping of my own—but in the quickest move I'd ever seen, he let go of my hair and had both my wrists in a single hand above my head.

Bishop slowly shook his head, clucking his tongue. "You aren't rushing me, Adler. I'm taking my sweet time with you, and you're going to love every fucking second."

Jesus fucking Christ. He hadn't even touched me yet, and I was already panting. What was I going to do when he actually made contact with my skin? I found out a second later when a flash of white teeth nipped at my bottom lip just like I'd done to him. He soothed the sting a second later, kissing me until I strained against his hold.

I wanted to touch him, taste him, but also? I really wanted to know what his plans felt like. Bishop's free hand snaked under my T-shirt, and gentle fingertips skimmed the skin of my belly on their way to my breast. But he didn't just cup the flesh. No, his teasing fingers deftly maneuvered around my bra and plucked at my nipple before his mouth descended, capturing the sensitive, aching flesh between his lips.

Had my breasts ever ached before? That, I couldn't recall, but fuck if it didn't make me almost come out of my skin. When he quit kissing them and raked his teeth over the peak, I actually did let that moan go free. It was equal parts frustration and need—I needed more, but I also needed these clothes off and both his hands on me and—

"If I let you go, are you going to be good and stay still while I taste you?" he whispered against my mouth. I shivered in answer, barely able to rub two synapses together, let alone actually respond.

Did I want to be good? If it meant Bishop's head between my legs? Abso-fucking-lutely.

"I'm going to need the words, Adler. You going to be good for me and keep your hands on the door, or am I going to have to get creative?" He pressed his body into me then, the heat of him making me damn near mindless.

"Yes," I breathed—the best I could do given that I was about a millisecond from coming, and I hadn't even gotten my clothes off yet.

"Yes, what?" he asked, nipping at the skin of my neck just under my ear.

What's the question again? Oh, right.

"I'll be good." I was probably lying, but I wanted my clothes off and his mouth on me, and I'd pretty much sell my soul to make that happen.

He hummed against my skin like he didn't believe me, but he still brought my hands down, pressing my palms flat to the door. Then he got to work, unbuttoning my jeans and sliding them down my hips along with my underwear. A moment later, his hands were at the hem of my shirt, pulling that up and off, and before I knew it, he'd unclasped my bra and drew that away as well.

I was naked—completely and utterly naked—as he stood before me fully clothed, his black T-shirt stretched across his chest like I wanted to be.

"Remember what I said, Adler?"

He said something?

The corner of his mouth curled up into the most devilish of grins. I wanted to taste that mouth. I wanted that shirt off, those pants. But most of all? I needed him to touch me, or I would go insane.

He pressed into me again, the roughness of his clothing barely taking the edge off my need to be touched by this man. "Hands on the door. Now."

First, I needed to even locate my hands—which were

holding tight to his shirt like I wanted to rip it off—*I totally did want that*. Where they were not was on the stupid door. When exactly they had traversed the space between us, I wasn't sure. Nothing on my body was listening to my commands, only Bishop's because my palms found the door with no problem.

"Good girl. Now stay still."

The order made my whole body clench. I wasn't thinking about the ideas rolling around in his mind or what had transpired in the last few weeks. All I could feel was his lips as they trailed down my sternum to my belly and lower. All I could hear were my own ragged breaths. All I could see was his golden eyes and broad shoulders and perfectly fucked-up hair that practically begged me to run my fingers through it. All I could smell was his smoky scent. I wanted to bathe in it, roll around in it. I wanted it all around me.

When his lips finally reached my center, I lost the fight, my fingers finding their way in his hair. The soft strands tickled my palms as his tongue stroked through my folds, circling my clit with such a blinding heat, I thought I was going to pass out. His fingers slid inside me, making my knees buckle, and then I wasn't standing anymore. One second, I was trying to stay vertical, and the next, I was flat on my back on my living room rug as he devoured me.

He was relentless, wringing pleasure from my body like he owned it. Sounds I had no idea I could make fell from my lips as heat washed over my skin like a flash fire. My release hit with the force of a fucking bomb. The world could have exploded for all I cared.

I came back to myself just in time to watch Bishop rip his shirt over his head. Smooth golden skin was all I could see, and I wanted it. It didn't make any sense. I should've wanted to sleep for a week after what he'd just done to me, but instead, I needed his scent in my nose and my lips on his skin. But the sight of his fingers working his belt was also something I needed. His deft fingers—the ones that had just been inside me —oh, so slowly maneuvered the leather. Those same fingers that had grazed my clit with such expert skill, unbuttoned the top of his jeans and yanked his zipper down.

Sitting up, I reached for him, snaking my hands inside the band of his briefs, and yanked. It took a few good pulls to unearth my prize, but before I could wrap my fingers or mouth around him, Bishop had my face in his hands and his mouth on mine, the taste of my arousal still on his tongue. Luckily, my hands needed little direction, finding the smooth, silky skin of his erection with minimal effort. Teasing him crossed my mind, but I just didn't have it in me. Instead, I glided my hands over his cock, the thrill of his hitched breath making me crazy.

"I want inside you. Fuck, baby, I need inside you so bad," he groaned against my mouth, the rough gravel of his voice touching me everywhere. He let go of my face, one hand going to my ass as the other sifted through my hair, his lips finding the tender skin of my neck.

"Yes," I moaned before finding his lips again.

And then we moved.

Somehow—because I wasn't exactly sure physics had an explanation for this one—he lifted me, and I went from my knees to my back in a single fluid movement, landing with Bishop in between my legs.

Well, *that* I could explain.

It was the fact that all this happened while I was kissing him like the world was ending the whole time.

Then the blunt head of his cock slid inside me, and the world could have actually been ending for all I noticed. I felt so full—full of his scent, of him—that when he pulled back, I actually whimpered. My legs wound around his waist of their own accord, probably making sure he wouldn't get away. My hands roamed his fevered skin as if they couldn't get enough of the feel of him.

When he drove inside me again, the pair of us let loose, matching needy groans, and something about that sound set *something* off, because soon, he was pumping inside me, hitting that one perfect spot like he was built just for me. He captured my mouth, swallowing my moans as he spun me into a frenzy.

I wanted to come—needed it, in fact—but a part of me never wanted this to end. Never wanted to be any farther from him than right at that moment. Wanted to stay connected just that way.

But then he changed the angle of his hips, hitting that spot in a way that made me gasp.

"Come for me," he rasped. "Please, baby."

It was likely the "please" that did it, because as soon as the word fell from his lips, I saw stars. No, not stars. Whole solar systems. Galaxies. The entire fucking universe. Pleasure bigger than I'd ever felt slammed into me so hard I could barely breathe.

As if he was waiting for me, he let loose, his thrusts hitting a fevered pace as his grip on me tightened. Burying his face in my neck, Bishop came on a harsh groan. The sound vibrated through me as if that solitary gravelly epithet touched every single millimeter of my skin. I tightened my limbs, holding him to me as we melted into each other, our ragged breaths the only sound in the room.

Eventually, we peeled ourselves from the floor and got cleaned up. And by cleaned up, I meant that we had slippery shower sex, followed by still-wet bedroom sex, and middle-of-the-night sleepy sex after that. Bishop was asleep, his large limbs wrapped around me as he cuddled into my back, his calloused hand cupping my breast as he breathed the intense sighs of deep rest. I should have been passed out, too, but even though I wanted to sleep, I did not.

No, I was thinking—an act I was pretty sure was forbidden for at least another six hours. I was thinking about the note still in its evidence bag that was sitting on my coffee table.

Gently, I pulled myself from Bishop's arms and quietly dressed, yanking on jeans and one of my dad's old Aerosmith T-shirts. I hugged the fabric to me, trying to get a whiff of his scent, but all that was left was the fresh smell of fabric softener.

The grief mounted in my throat as I wrapped my hair in a haphazard bun, trying and failing to keep the world-rocking tremors from consuming my entire house. I padded in the dark, afraid to turn on the lights for fear I'd explode them.

I needed to know what Essex had planned with that damn note, and I needed to know right then.

You know the saying about curiosity killing the cat?

Well, I was the cat.

3

I wasn't exactly sure how the evidence bag ended up in my hands. I couldn't actually recall picking it up or opening it, for that matter. Sure, I had about a zillion—give or take—souls just chilling under my skin, but breaking a Fae sealing spell should still totally be out of my wheelhouse.

Evidently, it was not.

The gold, glittery magic ripped like tissue paper, and I had that bag open without so much as a whisper.

Looking back, I knew I shouldn't have touched the card. I *knew* it. But something about the parchment called to me like a siren song, begging me to find out what my idiot brother was up to. Jimmy had said there was a dark spell weaved into the paper, that it was most likely meant to kill me, but I just couldn't stop myself from reaching inside the bag to touch it.

You know in scary movies, when you looked at the heroine and wondered how fucking stupid did they have to be to do something so obviously bad for them? So clearly against their own survival? So moronic that the fact that they had survived up to this point and hadn't choked on a marble or something was a fucking miracle?

That was me.

I was that dumb bitch.

"What are you doing?" Bishop asked right before my fingers made contact, the sheer force of the alarm in his tone making me hesitate for just a moment as I watched him pull a T-shirt over his head.

But I didn't answer him. What I was doing was painfully obvious—at least to me, it was. I was getting that note. After that, my plan was a mystery to the pair of us. In fact, I couldn't exactly call this a plan. This was more of a horrible need that doubled as the worst idea I'd ever had in my life. But more? It was as if I couldn't control my hand at all, like I wasn't in charge anymore.

"Darby, darling, I'm gonna need you to put that note down and take a giant step back. Can you do that for me?"

Meeting his gaze, I saw the instant he knew I couldn't do what he wanted. And I tried—I did—but I just couldn't make myself put the bag down no more than I could stop my hand's progress as it inched toward the cursed parchment. His eyes flashed gold as swirls of magic raced up his arms. The ground beneath our feet shook so hard I thought the whole house was going to break in half.

A siren's call of darkness pulled my gaze toward the paper, the curse swirling closer and closer to my flesh. And then I touched the parchment, the rough linen skating across my fingers as I latched onto the card with its dreadful inscription.

At first, I thought nothing happened—that I was immune to the curse that writhed like a den of snakes.

Then the pain hit.

I had a feeling being struck by lightning would have hurt less. Black needles of magic raced up my arm, the darkness of the curse rushing toward my heart at breakneck speed. The souls inside me raged in answer, fighting against the darkness as they roiled under my skin. I had no power, no say, the two forces colliding in war beneath my flesh. What had once been a dull rumble of souls was now a maelstrom of power doing anything it could to fight, anything to leave the pitiful prison that was my body.

I wanted to scream. Hell, I wanted to cry. I wanted to do anything but sit idly by as these two forces duked it out on the playing field that was my body. But instead, I collapsed, the utter agony too much to bear.

There was no slowing it down, no stopping it, no way to make it better.

Arms caught me as I fell. "Darby, baby. Please."

Shakily, I met Bishop's gaze, mouthing the name of the only person I thought could help me, "Azrael."

Then the darkness consumed me.

One would think that once you passed out, the pain would go away. If you were lucky, that's exactly what happened. If you were me? Not so much.

I hadn't been lucky a day in my life, and today was no different.

Blackness clouded my vision as the first convulsion hit, my body tightening hard enough that I thought my bones were going to snap. I couldn't speak. I couldn't see. I couldn't hear. All there was, was the pain. It could have been minutes or hours, days or years. All I knew was blistering agony with no release and no escape.

I would have gladly taken death at this point, but a part of me wondered if this was death. If this was Hell.

If this was my penance for the wrongs I'd done. Because I hadn't been able to save my dad. Because I had taken out my vengeance on those that hurt me. Because I'd taken lives.

Because more and more I felt like a monster.

And just when I thought it couldn't get any worse? My lungs stopped working. I tried and tried, but the air never reached my lungs, the burn of the lack of oxygen making everything that much more horrifying.

Please. Please, baby, just keep breathing. I'll do anything. I'll give you anything. I'll take you to Azrael. I'll take you anywhere. Just stay.

Bishop's words were like a light in the dark, a lifeline I couldn't quite grasp. Then it wasn't just Bishop in my head. It was Sloane and Bastian, their friends. They were clamoring, yelling—but not out loud.

It was their thoughts—their fears—rattling inside my head that made the pain just that much more unbearable, that much crueler.

Please. Please don't. I'll do anything. Don't make me leave her.

But Bishop's arms did leave me, the cold, dewy grass filtering through the burning maelstrom churning under my flesh.

I tried my hardest to reach for him—to tell him I was sorry, that I loved him, something—but before I could will my arms to move, Azrael's voice filtered through my brain.

Hang tight, you hear me, Darby? Don't you dare let go. I know you're in pain. I know you're tired. I'm going to make it better. Just...

But he never finished the thought. No, what happened next defied everything I thought I knew about death, about life, and about the fabric of who I was. But as much as I wanted to hold tight to the last shred of life I had within me, I was tired.

So tired.

Tired of losing and never getting a win.

Tired of always coming last.

Of failing. Of pain.

Intellectually, I knew I needed to hold on. Not only for me, but for Bishop, and J, and Sloane. For the friends and family I'd made. But it just didn't seem fair that I had to be the one to endure. Death couldn't be worse than this—there was no way. But just when I was about to let go, to give up, the first bit of relief hit me, pulling an ache straight from my chest like someone was sucking poison from a wound.

Here was something no one told me about pain: any relief, no matter how small, felt like the first drop of water after weeks without. It was bliss and agony all wrapped together—bliss because any relief was better than nothing, and agony because it just wasn't enough. Then it felt like someone reached into my chest and started ripping through everything soft, yanking and pulling, the burning, clawing torture so much worse than before.

I felt myself lifting from the ground, a blinding bright light slashing through the dark. But with that agony, I found my voice. And I screamed. I screamed loud and long and hard enough to shred my throat to ribbons.

Just a little bit longer. Almost there. Hang on, Darby.

Azrael's voice was not the balm it should have been, nor was it at all encouraging. Because I didn't have much left to hold on with—no energy, no strength, and for damn sure, no will.

The pain abated little by little, the relief just as disorienting as the agony had been, and soon it was replaced with what I could only assume was the normal level of pain. So basically, I went from "wanting to die" levels, to just "run over by a truck" levels.

Solid improvement.

It was the silence that struck me first. Before I'd touched that damned cursed note, everything had been so loud. Even in the midst of whatever Azrael had done, the dull roar of the trapped souls was so loud it was a wonder I could hear anything at all. In the grand scheme, I knew he'd done what I could not and expelled the souls locked inside me, but that knowledge took a bit too long to process for my liking.

It also took far too long to gather the strength to open my eyes, and even longer to focus on the face in front of me. Warm gold irises filtered through the haze first, then Bishop's wet cheeks that appeared just a shade too pale. It was the stillness from him that caught me off guard—his mind now closed to me as the power had been leached from my body. I was sorry to say I missed the cadence of his thoughts.

Bishop helped me sit up, and the world tilted a bit more than it should, and it again took far too long to understand. I was sitting in the grass, the blades scorched from a freshly extinguished fire. Just beyond the circle of Sloane's people, great cracks rent the earth, the jagged soil uneven and craggy.

This I understood.

My sister in the middle of this circle of destruction, I did not.

She knelt beside me, her body shivering in fear or cold or pain, I couldn't decipher which. Her hair was a mess, the white strands tangled and trailing down her back. No one looked at me—and I was fine with that—but the way they looked at Sloane made my whole gut pitch in dread, and I didn't think that was possible.

"Sloane?" I croaked, and she shifted to face me, her skin paler than it had been just hours before and tears quickly drying on her ravaged face. "What—what happened?"

My gaze flicked from Sloane's grim expression to her hands—her shaking hands that she clutched to her chest as if she was afraid someone might touch them. It took me a second to really see, though—to really get what Azrael had done. Honestly? It only took me catching a corner on a single sigil to know. I felt for the ring that had been resting at the base of my thumb, and I finally comprehended the full gravity of what Azrael had done to save me.

He saved me, yes.

But he'd damned her.

"Oh, no," I whispered stupidly, my eyes welling with equally stupid tears. "What did he do?"

Shrugging, she gave me a tremulous smile. "He didn't say."

But I knew. I knew because it was the most horrible thing I could think of—the thing I worried about and refused to accept. Those souls were inside my sister, and she would have to take them to the Underworld for me. Because I was too weak, too...

"No," Bastian growled, cupping my sister's face in his hands as he stared her down. "I'm going with you. You promised me, Sloane. Remember? You swore."

If my heart hadn't been breaking before, it sure as

shit was now. I couldn't keep my father because he'd already been raised from the dead. Sloane had raised Bastian. The implications of him following her to the Underworld weren't just awful.

They were tragic.

"What?" Simon whispered, that single word hissing from his lips like he was ready to breathe fire.

It made sense in more ways than I could count. Simon didn't want to lose his brother, I didn't want to lose my sister, and neither of us got a say.

Charging forward, Simon ripped Bastian away from Sloane, hauling the bigger man to his feet. The death mage's eyes went full black, so unlike Bishop's when he displayed his power. "Are you crazy? Is that it? Kick over and leave me behind? I don't bloody think so."

Bastian shook off his brother's hold, but Simon latched onto his arm again like a wayward barnacle. "Stay out of this, Simon. You know damn well you'd do the same for Dahlia. And there's no proof that arcaners have that same rule applied to them. I'm going, brother, and there is nothing you could say to stop me."

Thomas roughly pulled the brothers apart, shaking them like he was desperately trying not to pull a *Three Stooges* and knock their heads together. "Want to clue the rest of us in? Not everyone mind-melded with a death god, for fuck's sake."

For an ancient, Thomas really needed things spelled out for him. Those souls had to go somewhere, and that somewhere was not fucking *Disneyland*.

"Azrael is taking Sloane to the Underworld," Simon answered, his sneer seeming to mask the heartache that was also boring a hole in my chest. "My idiot brother wants to go with her, even though he most likely will be trapped down there." He ripped Thomas' hand off his flannel shirt and shoved Bastian's shoulder, adding a little of his power behind it, causing Bastian to stumble. "You promised me when Mum and Dad died that you wouldn't follow them. You're a liar, brother." Simon pointed a finger right at Bastian's face, a black swirl of magic racing up his arm. "You're a fucking liar."

Bastian pinched his brow as his shoulders hunched. "I made that promise when we were children, Simon. Tell me. If Dahlia were in the same position, would you let her go alone, knowing that she might be trapped there, too? Would you kiss her on the lips and bid her goodbye, knowing she might not come back to you? Or would you follow her and damn the consequences? Because living another thousand years without her would be the worst torture you could imagine?"

Simon staggered back as if Bastian had punched him in the gut. "It's not fair."

Dahlia grabbed his hand, threading her fingers through his. "It never is."

It was Simon's acceptance that hurt the most. He was going to lose his brother and I...

I was going to lose Sloane. I was going to lose her, and I'd just found her. I'd never get to know what she liked on pizza or what her favorite Halloween movie was. She'd never tell me what her parents were like or...

The question bubbled up my throat before I could stop it. "Why?" I whispered, still staring at her rapidly healing hands, the metallic sigils that had once been embedded in Azrael's ring, making themselves permanent in Sloane's flesh. "Why would he do this to you? After all you've lost."

After all we've lost.

Simon wiped at the tears on his cheeks before striding across the grass and pulling Sloane up by her arm. "He gave you an hour, and we've wasted enough of it. You have to get ready."

An hour? Azrael had only given her an hour? That knowledge ripped a hole right through me—one I was still recovering from while he dragged her toward the Night Watch mansion. She trailed behind him, and Bastian and the redheaded Clem followed fast on their heels.

"An hour?" I croaked, finally looking at Bishop again.

He'd been clutching me to him this whole time, and without him, I likely would have wilted right back into the grass and passed out.

His face said it all.

An hour. That's all she had. All they had.

And then she would be gone.

4

"Now, you are going to sit there and heal up, or I'll cuff you to the couch, you hear me?" Axel leveled me with his stern gaze as he handed off the saline bag to Dahlia so she could hang it on a thin rolling stand. "You get two bags of this and three more vials of Dahlia's tonic, and you're gonna let Clem feed you fried chicken and potatoes or so help me, I—"

"Yeah, yeah. Cuff me to the couch," I croaked. "You said that already. Where do you think I'm going to go? In case you missed it, I kind of had to be carried in here."

This was no exaggeration, either. After Simon dragged Sloane into the half-ruined house, Bishop hauled me into his arms and picked across the broken lawn after them, ordering Axel to check me over. At the time, the state of my health hadn't been a concern—at least not to me—but the ghoul had taken one look at me and raced to his medical bay to gather supplies. Dahlia had already shoved a vial of something disgusting down my throat—plugging my nose and force-feeding it to me and all. I wasn't too keen on taking another three of those damn things.

They tasted like charred feet.

"I've known you for less than a week, girlie, and in that time, you have done a whole heap of dumb shit. I don't rightly trust your judgment right now."

I needed him to get out of my face so I could get upstairs, and *what*, I couldn't exactly say. I was in no shape to do anything but stand by while my sister did the heavy lifting for me. And it sucked. A lot.

At the very least, I wanted to say goodbye. To hug her one more time. To tell her what meeting her had meant to me. It didn't seem like enough—none of it did—but it was something.

"If I pinky promise that I'll stay on the IV and drink those horrid healing tonics, will you do me a favor and quit bringing up how stupid I've been?"

Axel's warm brown eyes crinkled at the corners as his expression softened. "I can do that."

I held out my pinky to hook with his. He frowned at it. "What? You've never pinky promised before?"

The ghoul huffed a little chuckle. "I have. It's just I didn't think you were serious. Pinky promises are serious business."

If it got him to go somewhere else and not watch me like a hawk, then I'd vow my firstborn. I shook my hand, raising my eyebrows. He hooked it with his, doing an awkward little pinky shake.

Thomas approached, slapping the man on the arm. "Get your stuff, man."

Axel shot the vampire a grave look. "Yeah."

Fear crossed his expression for a moment before he nodded. He quit holding my pinky and nervously smoothed his hands down the front of his chambray shirt. Without so much as a nod toward an explanation, he hooked Dahlia's neck with one of his huge hands and pressed a kiss to her temple. Without another word, he pivoted on a heel and marched up the stairs.

Thomas didn't follow him right away. Instead, he knelt at my side and took my hand in his. I didn't know what he would say, but my gut told me it couldn't be good.

"I'm going to look out for your sister, Darby. I'll make sure she's safe."

There was nothing in Thomas' expression that told

of his love for my sister. Not even an inkling of the real reason he was going, or why he'd follow a woman, who didn't love him, all the way to Hell. I hated that his mind was closed to me now, hated that I didn't know if he was doing this for her or himself.

But it didn't matter. If he followed through and kept my sister breathing? Well, that was all I cared about.

"Good." I mean, what else could I say? There was nothing else, and dissuading him would be more pointless than tits on a bull. And if I actually managed to convince him to stay and she died? Well, I was pretty sure neither of us would forgive me.

Thomas nodded as he stood, and then he was gone, racing up the stairs behind Axel like the hounds of Hell were chasing him.

Dahlia shoved a blue bottle in my hand, the stopper conveniently gone. "Bottoms up," she muttered, wiping at her cheeks like she was mad at the tears that deigned to fall. "Don't make me force it down your throat this time, either."

"This sucks, doesn't it?"

She huffed, rolling her eyes. "Not everything can taste like bubblegum and jelly beans, Darby."

I shook my head. "You know that's not what I mean."

Her answering smile was more of a grimace than anything else. "Yeah. It sucks."

"Do you think she'll come back?" I asked, the faint whisper of my words more of a plea than anything else.

Dahlia blinked before she lifted her eyes to the ceiling. Pieces of it were still cracked and jagged, much like how we all felt. "I hope so. I hope they both come back, but..."

No one knew better than I did that what I hoped and what panned out wasn't exactly similar.

Bishop and Emrys walked shoulder to shoulder down the stairs, Harper trailing them. None of them had happy expressions on their faces. Emrys and Harper peeled off, but Bishop came right to me. Dahlia handed him the two other vials, following Harper into the dining room.

Bishop pressed his lips together, his grim expression not wavering an inch. He was going to tell me something terrible, I just knew it. But instead of saying anything at all, he sat next to my covered feet. He pulled them onto his lap, squeezing the tips of my toes and running his thumb along the line of my arch.

My eyes wanted to roll into the back of my head. Everything hurt—literally everything. From the tips of my toes to the follicles of my hair—all of it had the distinct feeling of being on Death's doorstep. But that single thumb rub? Solid ten-point-five on the happy scale.

But as good as it felt, and how happy it made me that despite my raging dumbness, we'd both made it out alive—more or less—I still wanted him to leave me alone. I still wanted to race upstairs and find my sister and hug her for what I hoped wouldn't be the last time.

Gathering my gumption, I brought the blue vial to my lips and chugged it back like a shot. Where was salt and a lime when you needed it? I held out my hand for the next bottle. Bishop yanked out the stopper, and I tossed it back, damn near gagging this time.

I coughed and had to fight off a full-body shudder that managed to hurt my bones. I waved for him to give me the last one, tossing that down my gullet, too. If college me could see me now.

The awful thing about those potions? They weren't helping me. Four healing tonics should have made me walk on freaking air. Right then, I couldn't even think about walking, or it would make my stomach pitch. I wasn't getting up those stairs without help, that was for damn sure.

"Whatever it is, it's bad, isn't it?" I muttered, reaching for Bishop's hand.

He took my fingers in his and stared at them instead of me, the line of his jaw a granite slab. "Yeah."

I wasn't healing, Sloane was going to the Underworld, and there was something more, something he wasn't telling me.

Something bad.

"Do you think you could take me upstairs so I can say goodbye to her?" If this was it—the last time I saw her—I didn't want to steal away and hurt myself again. I didn't want to hurt him by doing another dumb thing. And I sure as shit didn't want to lie.

He stared at my fingers—the same ones that Axel had complained were too cold and not reacting to pressure appropriately. "Do you think that's wise?"

I sighed. "Probably not, but I don't have time to debate it. She's leaving, Bishop. Maybe forever. I—"

The words got clogged in my throat, and I didn't finish my sentence. *I don't want another person in my life to leave and not get to say goodbye.*

He brought my fingers to his mouth and kissed them. Then he let them go and nodded like he had come to some sort of decision. He tilted to the side and slid one arm behind my back and the other under my knees, and up we went, blanket and all.

"Grab the saline," he murmured, and I released it from its metal hook. Then we were off, hiking up the stairs together. Or more like he carried me and my pitiful ass up the plush carpeted stairs like a damn toddler, but whatever.

At first, I didn't know which room we needed to go to, but then I heard Thomas' patented growl. "You plan on stopping us?"

I wiggled in Bishop's hold, and he set me on my feet. Saline bag in hand, I took off. Okay, I hobbled as if every bone from the waist down was broken, while the air in my lungs felt like napalm.

"Don't go yet," I called, nearly tripping on a stack of books as I rounded the corner to a torch-lit room straight out of a torture nightmare. The walls were a dark-gray stone that seemed both wet and dusty and lined with large shelves filled with hefty tomes. There was a table at the center of the room with bottles, shrunken heads, and sharp implements stained with who knew what.

Sloane, Bastian, Thomas, and Axel stood on one side of the room, Azrael in the middle, and Simon on the other side, his finger pointing to a line of text in his book like he was marking his spot. Everyone had a bristled look about them, like they were about to duke it out in the middle of the floor.

But it was the feel of the room that struck me the most. Deep down in my aching bones, I knew this was the precipice to something, an entrance, a crack in the fabric of what was real.

Then it all became clear. This place was the entrance to the Underworld. Somewhere beyond these walls was all the dead, every soul.

Dad. That knowledge yanked at my stomach, pulling it into a freefall.

"You're supposed to be resting," Axel growled, pinching his brow. "I could have sworn I told you to stay hooked up to that IV and down Dahlia's herbal remedy. Are you ignoring everything everyone is saying today, or is it just me?"

I had the urge to stick my tongue out at him but stopped myself. Instead, I straightened my spine as I held up the saline bag in my hand, the same one that was filtering freezing liquid into my veins at breakneck speed. "I'm still hooked up, but if you think I'm letting ya'll leave without me hugging my sister—especially after she saved my fucking life—well, I can't fix that level of stupid."

I marched toward my sister—okay, so it was a pitiful hobble—and reached for her hands as I tried to catalog every single angle of her face. "You know, I thought I wouldn't miss reading everyone's thoughts, but right now, I kind of wish I still could." I opened my mouth as stupid tears filled my eyes. Dahlia was right. This wasn't fair. "I'm sorry you have to do this. I'm sorry you have to fight this battle for me. I'm—"

She cut me off with a gentle hug like she was afraid she would break me. Hell, she probably could. "I don't blame you. I wouldn't ever blame you. And, hey. Maybe I'll look in on Killian for you," she offered. "Tell him you said hi."

That broke me, and I clutched her to me with all the strength I had left. This was so much worse than I thought it was going to be.

"If you see him, can you tell him he was a wonderful dad for me? And then come back, okay? But if it's a question, I'd rather you just come back."

And that was the biggest truth of them all. Yes, I wanted to know if Essex was lying, but more? I wanted my sister to come back. I wanted her to live and have a future and happiness. So much happiness.

"Now get moving so you can be home before I know it or some other timey-wimey bullshit," I muttered, gathering myself and pulling away so they could leave. Axel had informed me of how time was supposed to work in the Underworld, and it didn't make that first lick of sense.

"What? No hug for me?" Azrael rumbled before speaking inside my head. *She's coming back to you, Darby. I wouldn't do that to you—take them both from you. It'll all work out. I promise.*

All I could do was stare at him, the betrayal of putting my sister in this position still at the forefront of my mind.

You see that you do. You bring her back to me alive and whole, and we'll be square. You keep her safe, and I'll forgive you. I'll do whatever you need me to do, just…

I will, Darby.

I held out my hand to shake, and he stared at my hand before giving it a wry smile. He took it in both of his own.

It's a deal, then. Azrael's voice was soft in my head, almost loving, reminding me of my dad in a way that made it hurt to breathe.

Then he pulled me to him, pressing a kiss to my forehead.

I love you, kid.

But it wasn't the "I love you" that made me nearly sag to the floor. No, as soon as his lips touched my head, the pain in my body went away. Every aching breath and grinding bone, every muscle spasm and burning agony faded. I wrapped my arms around his waist, squeezing him in the first real hug we ever had.

Thank you. I don't know what you just did, but thank you.

He squeezed me back. *I righted a wrong. You and your*

sister shouldn't have had to do this, and I'm sorry about that. Just know that it'll make sense soon. I love you, Darby. Take care of yourself, will you?

It sounded like he was saying goodbye, and for some reason, that hurt just as bad as the pain he'd just taken away had. I drew away, meeting his gaze for the barest of moments. He was blurry, so I dashed the tears from my eyes and studied him—memorizing him, too.

Because Azrael would do everything in his power to make sure Sloane came back—even if that meant dying himself.

5

Retreating seemed like the coward's way out, but that was precisely what I did. As soon as I broke that hug with Azrael, I raced from the room—unable to keep my tears in for one more second. Naturally, my retreat was hindered by Bishop, his strong arms catching me just as I turned the corner into Simon's room.

They were leaving, and I couldn't watch either of them go.

"Shh, baby," Bishop whispered into my hair as he held me tight.

Staggered breaths left my lungs as I tried to hold everything in. "They're... they're..."

What I planned to tell him, I didn't know. What could I say that he didn't know already?

Bishop pulled away, cupping my jaw in his hands. His thumbs brushed away the wet on my cheeks. I hesitantly met his gaze, those beautiful brown eyes staring back at me instead of the gold. "They're leaving?"

I nodded, a lump of sorrow stealing my voice. It didn't matter that I no longer felt like I was knocking on Death's door, my heart wouldn't survive this if...

"That's good. I'm glad they'll get out of here in time."

My whole body froze. "Wait, what? In time for what?"

Instead of answering me right away, Bishop kissed my temple—a gesture that did not give me the likely intended warm and fuzzies. Then he pulled back, his eyes flashing gold. "He really did it. He really did it. He healed you. You don't smell like you're inches from death anymore."

I took a step back, putting a hand to his middle. "I might love you, Bishop La Roux, but if you don't start talking, I'm going to knock your ass into next week. What don't I know?"

He shook his head. "Azrael—he told me things would be okay." He reached out a hand and captured a strand of my hair, curling it around his finger. The strand was no longer blonde, but white just like Sloane's. I tried *really* hard not to freak out and remain focused on something other than my hair color. "He said that *you* would be all right, and considering we have the ABI knocking on our door, you being upright is *kind* of a good thing."

That had me taking another step backward. "The ABI is *what?*"

Yes, it came out as a screech, and no, I'm not sorry.

Bishop winced. "Technically, they're about two hundred feet outside the ward. Since we made that thing about as spicy as we could, they're still having trouble even figuring out how to find us, let alone how to break in. But they will get in at some point."

Somehow, someway, I had a feeling this was my fault. "Let me guess—breaking the world is a no-no?" I'd been informed of my destruction. Bishop said that my house damn near broke in half. In the tumult, this house had suffered damage, too. Given the state of it and the yard, I figured I was the beacon drawing them here. Then something else occurred to me.

"Or is it *him?*" I meant Essex. Because why else would the ABI be at our door if he hadn't ordered it? *The fucker.*

Bishop shook his head as if he didn't know how to answer me.

The redheaded zombie that was Clem marched in the

room, a filled holster in one hand and a clinking canvas bag in the other. She offered me the gun and Bishop the bag. "Load up. You're left-handed like Sloane, right?"

I accepted the left-handed hip holster, confused as to how she knew my dominant hand but glad I at least had a weapon. "Yeah. Thanks. Ammo?"

My gut pitched and knotted with a bit of unease at the thought of getting in a gunfight—or any fight whatsoever—with the ABI, but if I was going to do it, I wanted to at least make it out the other side. Plus, if Essex had sent them—or was with them—I would make sure he never touched my sister, never reached the Underworld, and never hurt another person.

Not ever again.

"In the bag. Harper says that they've got a damn arsenal out there—maybe a syphoner or two," Clem replied, shuddering a little at the end.

Bishop sucked air in between his teeth. "Shit, I hope it isn't Eloise. Especially at this time of night. At this hour, she'd drop a ward out of spite."

I hadn't a clue who Eloise was, but I had a feeling if Bishop didn't want to contend with her, then she had to be formidable.

"*Damn* if I don't hate those kinds of witches. Stealing magic like that?" Clem shivered. "No, thank you."

Syphoners were a tricky bunch, and the politics

surrounding them in the community was sticky at best. Several covens shunned them because they stole magic, while others welcomed them because they could be used. Personally, I believed it depended on the witch, but I knew I stood in the minority on that issue.

But syphoner or not, I really only cared about one thing. "Is he out there? Is he with them?"

Because that was the real rub, wasn't it? Essex wanted the power of those souls. Would he follow Sloane to the Underworld to get it? Would he kill us all to find the way in? The answer to both of those questions was a solid "Yes."

Clem shook her head, wringing her hands against her black gingham dress as one of her red curls slipped from her careful updo, swinging with the motion. "I don't know. Harper didn't say."

I opened my mouth to ask another question when a crash rang out from the other room. All three of us raced back to Simon's lair to see a pale-faced Thomas hanging from Axel's arms as his legs gave up the ghost.

"Someone get me some blood bags," Axel growled, setting Thomas down. "Unless one of ya'll want to let him tap a vein."

"I'll go," Clem offered and bolted out of the room on her absurd heels.

"What happened?" Bishop asked as I knelt at Thomas' side.

His black eyes were run through with red, as if he was having trouble keeping his vampire side under control. Blood stained his lips, drops of it dribbling down his chin. He struggled to sit up, but Axel pressed one of his giant mitts against his chest and shoved him back down.

"This fool thought that not telling us Simon's spell hadn't worked on him was a good idea," Axel answered for him. "We didn't even make it out of that fool hallway before his years started catching up to him. I'm glad we started out walking, or else this idiot would be knee-deep in the Underworld and stuck since they don't let dead people just walk out willy-nilly."

Thomas had sworn to me that he would keep Sloane safe, and he couldn't keep that promise. That pit of dread that was in my belly? Well, now it had swallowed me whole. My sister was down two assets, and this did not make me happy at all. I felt like an asshole for thinking it, too, because Sloane actually gave a shit about Thomas. She cared if he lived or died.

Thomas gasped, coughing up more blood. Axel rolled him to his side so he wouldn't aspirate and freaking drown on his own fluids. I wanted to feel compassion—I swear. But all I could do was be pissed off that the ancient vamp might be giving up. It was written all over him. The set to his shoulders, the look on his face.

I don't think so.

"You're not taking the easy way out of this, you hear me?" I growled, grabbing the collar of his shirt and dragging him to sitting.

Was it absolutely idiotic to challenge a vampire that was older than Jesus himself? Probably.

Was I still doing it? Absolutely.

Because if there was a chance of us making it out of this, we were going to need everyone.

"You're going to breathe and live, and when those ABI fuckers inevitably break down the ward, you're going to fight with us. You're going to keep my sister safe like you promised and guard this damn door."

Thomas' eyes flashed with indignation, but I tightened my hold on his collar, my face far closer to an apex predator than was optimal for my health. Clem raced back in the room with an armload of blood bags, and I let him go so I could snatch one and shove it in his face. "Drink up, you old fart. We've got shit to do."

Thomas' eyes went full vamp-red as his needle-like fangs pierced the thick plastic. Blood bubbled up, and he sucked it down like a man—or rather, *vamp*—starved. *Good.* If Essex was outside, I needed him to get his ass in gear. I got busy donning the holster Clem had given me, while I eyed Thomas' progression through the blood bags. His color was returning, but not fast enough for my liking.

"What's this about the ABI?" Axel blurted, eyes wide, staring at me like I was a unicorn or something. He wasn't the only one. Axel, Bishop, and Simon were gawking at me like I just announced I was going to start stripping for lunch meat as payment.

I raised an eyebrow at Bishop, and he shook himself, filling in the rest of them on the scant knowledge we had. Listening in—and giving the stink-eye to Thomas, who was only on his fourth bag—I checked the gun Clem had provided. It was a standard M&P nine-mil that was modified for a lefty. If we made it out of here, I'd have to thank her for the consideration.

Seating my weapon, I checked on our ailing vampire again, only he wasn't exactly where I left him. In a blink, he was up and coming right at me. The fact that I could track the movement alone was a freaking miracle. That Bishop managed to work his half blood mage mojo on him before he reached me was another. I stared at the vampire from the other side of Bishop, eyes red and fangs on bloody display. Bishop's magic was its normal bright purple, the swirls of his power the only thing keeping Thomas at bay.

Great. That's all we needed—a pissed-off vampire who was mad I'd gotten him to stop his pity party.

Axel and Simon had a hold of Thomas' shirt, but the vamp just snapped his teeth at Bishop's magic as if he'd really enjoy burying those fangs in my throat. Hell, at some point, Clem must have run to get Dahlia, because the tiny witch had a ball of fire in her palm, like she was about to add napalm onto this shitshow of a tableau.

I craned my neck around Bishop, who was doing his best to keep me behind him. "Would you look at that? I guess you were right all along, Thomas. Antagonism really does get people off their asses."

The ancient vamp froze, making both Simon and Axel stumble. It was that same stillness that Ingrid sometimes did that freaked me all the way out. Slowly, he tilted his head, the snakelike movement cold and predatory. Now I had two options. I could shut up and pray he came back to himself, or I could double down and piss him off further.

Door number two, here I come.

"What? You don't like it when someone gives you a taste of your own medicine? Weird. I thought in two thousand years you would have learned how to sack up in that time, but I guess not."

An honest-to-god growl tore from his throat in

response, but all I did was shove down my fear and grin at the man.

"You're lucky I'm a gentleman," he snarled around his fangs. "Or else I would rip your throat out right now."

I scoffed, sneering right back at him. "Oh, you're such a gentleman? Is that why there are three men in between us?"

That remark had Thomas taking a step back from Bishop's magic. His eyes cleared of their red hue, and his fangs retreated. Had I known all it would take was impugning his honor, I would have done that sooner. "Point made."

"Actually," Simon interjected, "I was more afraid of what you'd do to him rather than what he'd do to you. Who bloody knows what Azrael did to you with that little forehead kiss? But for someone as in tune with the deceased as I am, I can venture a guess. You were damn near dead and then got a major power boost. Plus, have you seen your hair?"

I broke my vamp stare down to inspect the white locks. "Does it look bad?"

Both Simon and Dahlia rolled their eyes, but Dahlia was the one who answered, snuffing out the fire in her hand. "It looks beautiful, but that's not what he meant.

It's Azrael and Sloane's color, Angel of Death color. Who knows what little goodies Azrael gave you?"

I hadn't really thought about it but shrugged. "He's healed me before with no adverse effects."

Bishop's magic faded, and he shifted in my direction to give me a half-crazed look. "Has your hair ever turned white before?"

We both knew the answer was no, but we had bigger problems than the color of my hair—especially since Thomas appeared to be coming back to himself.

"So, are we gonna just stand here and pray the ABI doesn't beat down our door, or what?" Axel asked, rubbing at a bloody spot on his wrist. Thomas must have bitten him in the struggle.

"That's what I was coming in here to tell you," Dahlia said, slapping a wad of gauze on Axel's wound. "I had Clem go with Emrys and Harper. They're headed to the safe house. Emrys' contact said that they should be inside in a few minutes. We need to hold the line."

"Why aren't they holding the line with us?" Bishop grumbled.

Dahlia faced him, her eyes narrowed to slits. "Because if the ABI actually manages to breach the house, they'll try to use Harper as leverage against the rest of us. Emrys? They'll just lock her up. And Clem?

Well, they'll kill her on sight—and that's if they're playing nice. You know who you work for."

I knew the ABI wasn't exactly cupcakes and roses, but they'd just kill Clem?

I must have said this out loud because Bishop answered me, "She's a revenant—brought back by old magic they don't like. It's how Simon got put on house arrest for a century. The ABI doesn't deal too well with arcaners they don't sanction or ones they can't control. Clem is both—even if she is the most harmless zombie I've ever seen in my life."

"She's not a zombie," Simon muttered, clearly affronted. "She is a complex soul with—"

A rumble cut off Simon's words, the sound coming from the open door to the mansion.

That can't be good.

Bishop and Axel dove for the door, slamming the solid wood shut and shoving one of the heavy chairs under the knob. Sure, it wouldn't hold anything back, but it might make whoever was on the other side trip or something. Bishop, Dahlia, and Simon added a bit of their magic to an impromptu ward, though if the ABI had just blown through the massive one around the property, I didn't have high hopes of this one holding up any better.

Bishop grabbed my right hand, squeezing my fingers

in his. A year ago, I'd been trying to keep the ABI out of my life. Now, they might be busting down the door. I swallowed hard, a lump of fear making it difficult.

I met Bishop's gaze, his irises flashing gold as his brow pinched. He was just as worried as I was, and I couldn't blame him. We both knew just how ruthless the ABI could be—him more than me. If they would kill Clem just for being what she was, there wasn't much hope for the rest of us, now was there?

6

The rumble from the other side of the door had all of us taking a collective step back. It wouldn't take much time for the ABI to find us. Hell, if Essex was with them, our blood tie would make locating me a snap. The door rattled on its hinges, the ABI agents shouting from the other side that they were going to bust it down.

Shit.

How exactly were we going to get out of this? The only other way to go would be literal death, so it wasn't as if our options were all too plentiful. The door rattled again, the scant ward on the entrance holding for now, but it wouldn't for long.

It turned out the busting didn't come from the direction I thought it would. Instead of the warded door exploding to smithereens, a bookcase behind us took that honor. Books and wooden shards littered the floor as the dust settled, the concussion of the blast making everything muffled as a bedraggled man lurched out of the opening.

If it hadn't been for the white hair, I wouldn't have guessed who he was. The last time I saw Essex Drake, he had been sharp and composed—the smarmy bastard looking like he'd walked straight out of a fucking *GQ* advert. The man that staggered through the makeshift opening was bedraggled and limping, his cheeks hollow with dark purple bags beneath his eyes. His violet eyes flashed as they laser-locked onto me, a sneer of pure hate pulling his lips into a snarl. Essex roared as he dove for Simon's altar, snatching up a bloody cleaver and brandishing it at the closest person. Simon and Dahlia stumbled away from him, and the cold steel of my gun was in my hand before I ever told my hand to move.

The whole of the world slowed down in that instant, but it was as if I was moving at normal speed. Maybe it was almost a decade of training. Maybe it was that little boost I'd gotten from Azrael. Maybe I just really wanted to shoot him.

Well, I was sort of betting it was that last one.

The door behind me rattled and crashed, the sound of booted feet filling the room taking over my senses. I knew we—*I*—wouldn't have another opportunity to do this. If I wanted to end it—if I wanted to end *him*—this was my last chance. Without a second to consider the consequences, I aimed for his head and fired.

His big body veered off course, zigging when I expected him to zag, and the bullet hit his shoulder. Granted, it was the shoulder attached to the hand that had the giant fucking cleaver in it, but my intention was to kill, not maim.

I'm not Dobby, for fuck's sake.

Essex stumbled, dropping the cleaver with a clatter on the stone floor as a blur of wings and leather shot out of the corridor. The figure pivoted their body, landing like a giant bird on Essex's middle.

It took me a second to recognize the woman as she reached down and snatched him from the ground as if he weighed nothing. For one, my brain was trying to piece together how my sister got wings in the thirty minutes she'd been gone, and two? Sloane didn't exactly look like herself. Her skin glowed as if someone had switched a light on underneath her flesh. Her eyes flashed purple, and her fangs were twice as long as they had been before she'd left. Her hair gleamed white, her features just a little more beautiful, a little more alien.

She fisted her hand in the collar of Essex's shirt, similar to what I'd done to Thomas, only she did it with such gusto that he gasped like a fish out of water. She seemed like she'd really enjoy taking those extra-long fangs and ripping out his throat.

Too bad we now had a room full of ABI agents—one of which had a gun to my head and was taking my weapon.

"Sloane?" I breathed, hoping she would stop what she was doing and recognize we had company. She barely twitched as she moved closer and closer to Essex's throat. "Sloane!"

She shot me a baleful glare. "What? I'm a little busy here."

It seemed to take her a few seconds to register the giant ABI agent that was currently disarming me, my hands raised over my head in the universal sign for "Please don't shoot me." Her gaze trailed over the rest of the room, and I followed it. A couple of agents were frisking Simon and Dahlia for weapons, and a few others were clutching orbs of magic, prepared to throw them if we so much as flinched wrong. Thomas and Axel were pressed into the bookcase side by side as two men slapped magical cuffs on their wrists. Another agent pointed what appeared to be a modified paintball gun at Bastian. The canister was filled with glowing balls of liquid that had to be either a sleeping potion or something else altogether dangerous.

But what really pissed me off was how these agents were treating Bishop. They had him face-down on the floor with an agent's knee on his back and magical ropes around his arms, the twine digging so far into his skin, blood was welling around the fibers.

A short besuited gentleman—complete with a purple paisley tie—cleared his throat, stepping into the middle of the room like he was not only in charge, but he held our lives in the palm of his hand.

Maybe he did.

"As I stated before while you were otherwise indisposed: Arcane Bureau of Investigation. You're all under arrest."

The law-abiding side of me cringed, but the rebel in me was damn near giddy when Sloane started laughing —especially when he announced his name as if all of us were supposed to know who he was.

I mean, who in their right mind would be proud of a name like August Theodore Davenport, III? Sure, with the title of "Director" tacked on the front of it, it did sound official and all, but I doubted it mattered to her. There she was, wings spread, fangs drawn, holding up the Overseer of the Arcane Bureau of Investigation by his shirt collar like he was a child's toy. And this man thought she was going to listen to him?

Again, I doubted it.

"Fates, you are adorable," she said, wiping her eyes as tears of hilarity pooled in them. "Hate to break it to you, but unless your jurisdiction covers deities, you're shit out of luck."

A sinking feeling settled in my middle as I studied her wings. They looked just like Azrael's—the same black tips and smoky center. I tried not to think of why she had those wings, tried to focus on the small man with too much power, who so casually regarded my sister like she was gum on the bottom of his shoe.

"Deity?" Davenport scoffed. "And what deity are you supposed to be? The god of vampires? Or maybe you're one of those new gods that presides over avocado toast or something."

Davenport appeared to be no older than twenty, but based on the signature of power that surrounded him, he had to be much older. Still, that was a Boomer thing to say if I had ever heard one.

She flashed her fangs, her wings fluttering wide. "Tell me—have you ever heard of the Angel of Death? Don't answer that. I know you have. Well, Essex and I are his kids. He used to have a bunch, but Essex here killed them all. Even me. But see, Daddy didn't like that, and he brought me back." She turned her chin, staring Essex down as her fangs got closer and closer to his face. "All that power that you wanted, that you killed for, that you tried to steal? Belongs to me now."

I swallowed hard, trying to keep myself together as the reality hit me in a one-two punch of devastation. It wasn't that she'd kept my name out of her mouth when speaking of Azrael's children. No, it was her claim to his powers that hit the hardest. Because the question that screamed in my mind the loudest was, "Where was our father?"

Sloane returned her attention to Davenport. "So no, I won't be put under arrest, and neither will my friends. And Essex here, well, his time is up. I'm going to rip out his throat and watch him bleed. Then I'm going to chain his soul and haul his ass down to Tartarus. And if I see so much as a flicker of one of those spells, I'll take every single one of you down with him."

The other agents in the room seemed to get the message far faster than their boss. Their orbs of magic winked out of sight as the guns were properly stowed. Each one took a collective step back, and I couldn't say I blamed them. Hell, if Sloane weren't my sister, I'd be taking a step back, too.

"You can't be Death," Davenport countered as if he had the power to alter Fate, but Sloane only smiled, her eyes flashing brightly.

"I can, and I am."

He sputtered, shaking his head. "But Azrael—"

"Do. Not. Speak of my father as if you know him, *August*. You do not. I know in your precious little head, you think of him as a confidant or a shoulder to cry on, but I can assure you, Azrael is retired."

Retired.

A sob clawed its way up my throat. There was something wrong with Azrael. He was hurt, or he was... The expression on Sloane's face made me want to sink down to the floor and start bawling. We'd known each other for a week at most, but it was a look I'd seen a thousand times before. It was loss and pain and wrath all wrapped up into one expression.

Azrael wasn't retired. I was willing to bet that our father was hurt or dead—that last one wounding me in a way that I didn't believe was possible.

"I suggest you stand down, Director, and remember where you are." She gestured to the room at large. "This is the entrance to the Underworld. You're in my house, so to speak."

"But... but you're a murderer," he blurted, his hands balling into fists like a cranky toddler.

She scoffed and shot him a look of such contempt it was a wonder his hair didn't light on fire. "So are you, but if it makes you feel better, think of it as on-the-job training."

Davenport sputtered, damn near apoplectic. "You can't kill him. We need him."

"Oh, I assure you, I can, and I will." She tilted her head as if she was staring into his soul. "But what, pray tell, do you need this miserable, lying, murdering sack of dog shit for? Plan to install him in your newest ABI branch and let him run amuck? Maybe kill a few more agents, break a few more prisoners out of jail, conspire with Director O'Shea to open a goddamn rift in the planet so she can steal the power of the dead? What the fuck could you need him for?"

Davenport's shoulders fell in defeat. "He has answers. Knows who's dirty. Who's been bribed to keep their mouths shut. He knows where the bodies are buried."

Sloane snorted, shaking her head as she tightened her fist on Essex's collar. "No deal, sorry. I've seen the way your agency runs its prisons, and they leave something to be desired. You can't keep hold of the prisoners you've got."

Davenport sneered like she'd offended him. "Essex Drake would not be going to prison. He would go to a black site, sedated with enough sleeping potion to kill a fucking rhino, and strapped to a table until his brain has been mined of every detail, secret, and cover-up for the last four centuries. Then, you may do with him what you wish."

Sloane chuckled. "I can do what I wish now. What's in it for me?"

Davenport growled under his breath. Hell, if he had stomped his foot, I wouldn't have put it past him.

"Fine," he ground out. "I will expunge the records of Agents Bishop La Roux and Sarina Kenzari, releasing them from their contracts if they so wish. I will grant immunity to Darby Adler for her crimes against the Knoxville coven and the Monroe nest. She will be deputized as the new Warden of Knoxville and will accept the duties that entails."

Wait, what? Warden?

But he continued as if he didn't just kick over my life with his polished loafer. "Also, I will grant blanket immunities for all past crimes to Sebastian and Simon Cartwright, Dahlia St. James, Harper Jones, Axel Monroe, Thomas Gao, Emrys Zane, and that little revenant girl ya'll keep in the kitchen."

Sloane smiled at him like he was cute. "Get it to me in writing within the hour. Binding contract that states you may not have possession of Essex Drake for longer than one month, his body and soul to be claimed by me and only me."

"Done," he replied like the deal was already done.

"And Davenport?" she called softly, causing his shoulders to hunch all on their own. "One more thing."

"Yes?" Was that a whine I heard in Davenport's voice, or was it just me?

"The ABI will publicly acknowledge every agent and civilian Essex Drake has murdered, and you *will* pay their surviving families' reparations for up to one century."

Davenport's skin bled of color. "But—"

Sloane raised a single eyebrow at him.

"Fine," he said on a sigh. "You have a deal. Anything else you want to tack on? A pony, maybe?"

That was when I finally found my voice. "I want to circle back to what the fuck this Warden business is. Because I'd honestly rather put a bullet in his brain and go to jail than work for your smarmy ass. Offense totally intended."

Davenport regarded me with a wry grin. "They told me you were like this. I'm so glad the rumors are true. The Warden position is nonnegotiable, and you won't be working *for* me. You will be the intermediary between the ABI and the arcane populace of Knoxville—investigating crimes as you normally would, only with benefits and pay."

The rage coursing through me seemed to double as I

met Davenport's icy stare. "And in your pocket? No thanks."

His wry smile morphed into one that told me he thought I was adorable. "Not *my* pocket. The Arcane Council. And you can tell them no if you want to, but I wouldn't advise it."

Well, that just cleared everything right up.

7

Considering I hadn't heard of any Arcane Council before today, the timing of all of this seemed more than a little suspicious. Before I could call Davenport out on his bullshit, though, Sloane answered him for me.

"She'll take the position, go draw up the papers. I'll be holding Essex as collateral, so don't drag your feet."

Davenport ground his teeth. "Fine. Try not to kill him before I get back."

Sloane shrugged, her smile practically demonic. "I'll do my best."

The director sighed and took one of the odd paintball guns from an agent, pointed it at Essex, and fired five rounds, each hitting him center mass. Essex's eyes rolled up in his head as the potion balls did their job. He hung from Sloane's grip for a moment before she unceremoniously dropped him. I was pretty sure the smile that bloomed over her lips matched mine as the sickening thud of his skull meeting the stone echoed through the almost silent room.

Then Davenport snapped his fingers, the action conjuring barbed ropes from thin air. They twined around Essex's ankles, wrists, and the top of his arms, binding him like a damn mummy. The barbs pierced his flesh all at once, punching through his clothes and skin as blood welled from the wounds.

"There," the director said on a sigh. "This way, when I come back, the bastard might just be in one piece."

Sloane narrowed her eyes at the man. Grumbling, he snapped his fingers again, and the bonds that held Bishop, Thomas, and Axel fell away. Then Davenport and his agents swept from the room as they'd come in, with a rumble of booted feet and slamming doors. Personally, I was still stuck on the fact that my sister had answered for me, telling that absolute cream puff of a man that I would take a job I absolutely was *not* going to take.

"What the fuck, Sloane?" That "What the fuck" encompassed a lot of things. What happened? Are you okay? Where the fuck is Azrael? Why do you have wings? Why did you tell that fucking imbecile I was taking a job? That last one encompassed the forefront of my brain.

Sloane winced, her wings shivering as she tried to tuck them in and failed miserably. "We need to talk."

No *shit*, we needed to talk, but I kept that to myself as I inched closer to the man that had tried to kill me more times than I could count. It didn't matter if he was unconscious and bound—being this close to him made my stomach turn.

Sloane reached for my hand and placed a creased piece of paper in the center of my palm. "I'm doing this in a good news, bad news, good news sandwich for you because there isn't a lot of time."

I wanted to meet her gaze, but I was stuck on the folded note on my palm. It was familiar, as if it had been torn right out of one of my dad's legal pads. The yellow paper crinkled in my hand, my fingers closing over it like it was a treasure I wanted to keep safe. I didn't know if I was ever going to be able to read it. Hell, I could barely hold it without crying. Swallowing hard, I stuffed the note in my pocket.

"Killian wanted me to give that to you. He's okay— safe in Elysium. I met with him before…"

A tear raced down my cheek before I could stop it. "Before you lost Azrael," I croaked. "That's what you wanted to say, right?"

I managed to peel my gaze from my pocket to meet Sloane's eyes. Her glowing violet gaze hurt my heart. "Yeah," she whispered. "He saved us both. Saved Bastian —put himself between Essex and—"

Shaking my head, I awkwardly wrapped my arms around her, the wings making the hug more difficult than I thought it would be. "He kept his promise then."

Sloane chuckled wetly, her shoulders heaving a little before she pushed away. She dashed the tears on her cheeks. "That leads me to the other bit of not-so-good news. You have to take that job."

I took a step back, ready to lay into my sister, but she held a hand up.

"I know, but hear me out. You remember when Azrael would be super vague and not tell you anything? Well, it was because he *had* to. But in this one instance, I'm going to toss that bullshit out the window and give you a hint. You have to take this job. What's coming? I can't help you with it, and I can't fix it. Not taking this job? The outcome will be a hell of a lot worse."

I'd never had an urge to punch my sister, but I really did then.

"Jesus." Wincing, she rubbed her temple. "Your mind is crazy loud, you know that? I get it—I do—but things are different now. Azrael gave me all the power he had left, and with it, came a boatload of knowledge that I am not allowed to tell you about. I know we thought we couldn't trust him, but trust me, and take the job. Lives depend on it."

Her gaze flicked from me to the side, and I followed it as it landed on Bishop. He rubbed at his wrists and shoulders, which were still bloody from Davenport's bullshit barbs.

"Okay," I murmured, still staring at the man I loved more than I thought possible. The same man who'd saved me more times than I could count. "I'll take the job."

"Good. That makes my job a fuck of a lot easier."

It actually dawned on me that my sister was the new Angel of Death. I mean, sure, I *knew*, but I hadn't really put it together. "Can you really see the future like Azrael could?"

Sloane smiled and waggled her hand. "Yes and no—which is, again, vague as shit, but that's the best answer I can give. This crap is confusing and a lot, and... I'll get the hang of it soon enough."

"Are you sticking around?" Yes, my voice was that small, and yes, I sounded like a damn child, but losing people was not a habit I wanted to make.

She gave me a wry grin. "I'll be around, but we have to go back soon. I have business to deal with, and someone needs to teach me how to put these damn wings away. I feel the call to go back, so as soon as Essex is transferred, I'll have to leave."

I wanted to protest but knew better. Sloane's role had changed drastically, and I needed to let her go. Nodding, I gave her another awkward hug and stepped back, maneuvering past her so she could see everyone else. As soon as Sloane finagled her enormous wings around Simon's death table, Dahlia and Simon both attack-hugged her. Hell, Axel and Thomas piled on, too, the massive group hug a thing of beauty.

A second later, I was enveloped in my own attack-hug. Bishop wrapped me in his arms and squeezed tight. That squeeze made my eyes well up in frustrated tears, my emotions all over the place. I couldn't believe how his own brethren treated him, or the essential "Get out of jail free" cards we'd both been dealt. It made me sick to my stomach and giddy all at the same time.

"Nice shooting, Adler," he muttered in my ear as he sifted his fingers through my hair.

"Not nice enough," I grumbled. "The bastard's still alive."

Bishop shrugged, shifting us both so we could keep an eye on the definitely still-sleeping prisoner. Essex had been a boogeyman for so long, it was weird to see him trussed up like a Thanksgiving turkey.

"Not for long, and if him breathing gets us pardons, well, I'm all for happy accidents."

Bishop was free to leave the ABI now if he wanted. Free. What did that word even mean? "Are you—"

"Going to quit? Absolutely. Just as soon as I look that pardon over to make sure there aren't any loopholes to quitting. The last thing I want is to be caught up in some more bullshit."

My stomach dropped a little at his cavalier attitude. Bishop could go anywhere—do anything. He wouldn't be tied to Knoxville anymore.

"Just wait until I tell Sarina—though, the little shit probably knows. Hell, I wouldn't be surprised if she told Davenport what Sloane would agree to before he even announced the deal. He had to have had some prompting to list all that shit at once."

All I could do was nod. It totally made sense. Sarina was an oracle, after all. She likely warned Davenport of precisely that, and he was just the type to try to go against it.

Bishop pressed his forehead against mine. "And Warden? Knoxville hasn't had one of those in centuries. I can't believe it."

I pushed away to stare at him. "You actually know what this job is?"

He chuckled and reeled me back in. "Yes. It's sort of

like an arcane sheriff. There was one about three hundred years ago when the Europeans were causing a stink in the area. The populace lost faith in the ABI and was close to going to war. The council installed a Warden to keep the peace. It's an honor to be chosen. Given your in with most of the factions, maybe that's why I was sent to scout you in the first place. Mariana probably wanted to block the nomination to keep her seat of power."

Almost a year ago, Bishop had been sent to look me over. His boss thought I was trying to make a power grab for Knoxville. At the time, I hadn't known his boss had been my mother, and he hadn't known I was in the dark about her living status.

What a difference a year made.

"'Amassing an army,' wasn't that what you said?" I muttered, quoting his initial sales pitch as we searched for a killer. "Who knew all it took was killing a bunch of people to get the job, huh?"

Was that bitterness in my voice? Nah. Couldn't be. What call did I have to be bitter? Who wouldn't want their entire life to be thrown into the shredder?

"But you didn't. In their eyes, you didn't kill tons of arcaners. These are people who have fought in the oldest of wars—ones that decimated cities. You were methodical, thorough. Damn near surgical with how few lives were lost. Mariana was going to open a hole in the world. She was not only going to anger the gods. She was going to expose all of us to the humans. There would have been millions dead. Millions. You stopped her. These charges Davenport would have filed? They never would have seen the light of day. The council would have taken his head first."

As good as those words were to hear, it still didn't make sense to me. "Who is this council? You talk like you know who they are, but I've never heard of them before today."

Simon snorted as he approached, hands in his pockets, and beanie firmly planted on his head. "They are a secretive bunch of buggers that's for sure. Though Emrys used to be one of them once upon a time, so that makes complete sense. Unless you've done something either very good or very naughty, most people never even know the council exists. Sure, you hear whispers about secret societies and whatnot, but no one knows."

I could totally see Sloane's former boss as a shady councilmember. Hell, the way she sat in a chair had the air of being someone more than a little important. Bishop rolled his eyes and put a hand on the other mage's chest, playfully shoving him away from our conversation. Simon shot him a grin and ambled off to go talk to his brother.

"They are made up of the oldest arcaners," Bishop continued. "Not every faction has a seat—not all of them want one—but most of them do. I think it's a way to keep the ABI in line."

I could appreciate checks and balances as much as the next girl, but that still didn't tell me much. But something told me Bishop was holding back. I'd have to pick his brain later when there were less ears.

Bishop reached for my hand, threading his fingers with mine. "Warden," he whispered as if he was in awe of me. "You think you'll need a deputy or something? An assistant?" He reeled me in, wrapping his other arm around my lower back. "I saw that face you made earlier. I'm not going anywhere, Adler. ABI or not, you're stuck with me."

It was tough not to let a sigh of relief gust out of me, but I managed it. Though, I mucked it up with mushy words a second later, so the jig was up.

"I like being stuck with you."

"Good. So, when I turn in my paperwork, you won't freak out that I'll take off to parts unknown now?"

Could this man read me so well that he saw that very thought on my face? I really hoped not.

"I wasn't worried," I lied, ducking my head.

Bishop chuckled. "Sure you weren't, Adler. And

when I go with Davenport to supervise the transfer? You going to worry then?"

I squirmed. "No."

He hooked a finger under my chin, making my retreat impossible. "That's good because I'll see you right after. Okay?"

I nodded, the relief hitting me square in the chest. That relief might irritate the shit out of me, but the fact that Bishop knew I needed that reassurance pissed me off more. Man, I was messed up.

Like holy fucking abandonment issues, Batman.

Bishop was going to quit the ABI and stay. I marveled at the concept, still miffed it brought me so much damn joy.

Now I just had to decide whether or not I'd be handing in my badge as well.

8

Essex's transfer went smoother than I thought it would. Davenport returned without all the pomp and circumstance, brandishing the pardon papers for each of us as if he was waving the white flag of surrender. Sloane looked them over before handing them to Thomas. The ancient vampire perused the documents, red pen in hand, but made no changes.

After the documents were signed—which was really a bloody thumbprint from both Davenport and Sloane—the director took the prisoner. Bishop quickly followed, vowing to supervise the transfer.

A part of me didn't want to let him go—worried that somehow Essex could wake and kill them all—but I managed to keep my trap shut as I watched him leave.

I also wondered how I was supposed to get back

home. It wasn't like there were Ubers out here in the ass end of nowhere. I supposed I could call J to come pick me up, but then I'd have to explain just how I'd gotten here and what had happened, and that made my brain hurt.

How could I explain to my best friend that I'd lost another parent, had about a zillion souls extracted from my body, had epic sex with my boyfriend for the first time, and managed to shoot my brother all in the same night? Obviously, it wasn't in that order, but that story time was going to require about a fifth of vodka and enough tacos to kill a rhino.

And even then, I'd have to unpack my trauma, and I didn't want to. Sure, I'd have to do it eventually, but I sure as hell wasn't going to right then.

"You know someone would let you borrow their car, right?" Sloane whispered, startling me out of my internal dilemma. "But if you think stewing in avoidance is more important, by all means, keep going."

I fought off the urge to flip her off. "I am consciously avoiding my trauma. Let me, will you?"

Her wings shivered as she bumped me with her hip. "As you wish. I need to go."

My jaw clenched as I tried not to freak out. Sloane was going back to the Underworld. She was really going to be the new Angel of Death. Technically she already was, but I was still processing that *not*-so-little nugget. Things were changing far faster than I was ready for.

"Give me a hug," she muttered, wrapping her arms around me before I had a chance to respond. She squeezed tight, and I did the same. "Remember that I'll come if you call, so don't be a stranger, deal?"

Swallowing hard, I croaked, "Deal."

As soon as she broke off, she and Bastian clasped hands, winking out of sight, much like Azrael always had—there and gone in and instant. Almost as instantly, I felt out of place, awkward, and faced with the choice of asking someone to borrow their car or calling my best friend.

Both options seemed like shit.

"Here," Dahlia said, offering me a ring of keys from her index finger. "You can borrow my car. It's the blue Audi."

Gratefully, I took the keys, ridiculously happy I didn't have to ask. "Thank you. That is so kind."

Dahlia held up a hand. "Don't worry about it. I'll have Simon collect it tomorrow. I'd have offered to lend him out, but I know how much shade jumping sucks, so I won't bother."

I shuddered at the thought. Bishop had taken me shade jumping with him far too many times, and each time the experience was supremely fucktacular. "Again, thanks."

She led me to the garage and to the beautiful blue sports car. Honestly, I was a little afraid to touch it, but the alternative had me jumping in the thing like my ass was on fire. Okay, jumping wasn't on the menu since I had to adjust the seat so far back, but I made it work.

Before long, I was racing down the dark lane toward home, relying on the vehicle's GPS, given that I wasn't exactly sure where I was. The quiet filled me and I managed to turn my brain off for a few minutes, allowing the road to guide me. The sun crested the horizon, lighting my path as I raced toward Haunted Peak, but it wasn't until I turned off the car that I realized I hadn't made it to my house at all.

Frowning, I peeled myself from the seat as I stared at the cemetery before me. Haunted Peak Memorial Cemetery was located at the center of town and yet remained the least populated. Filled with very few ghosts and far too many cracked headstones, the graveyard had always called to me. I detested the popular Dove Creek Cemetery. In my youth I hated it because it had always been crawling with ghosts. Now I hated it because my father was buried there.

I struggled to swallow around the lump in my throat and shut the car door. I picked my way through overgrown weeds and over a pitiful chain that claimed the place was closed. This was where I'd spoken to Azrael for the first time, him appearing as a raven as he'd led me deeper among the graves. Following the path I'd taken what felt like weeks ago, I found myself at the headstone where he'd perched, the name worn away and half-covered in moss.

Before I thought better of it, I tried to brush a good bit of the moss away, the urge to know the name of the poor soul buried here damn near paramount. The urge didn't make a lick of sense, but a part of me connected this grave to Azrael. It was a monument, a touchstone, a place where I could come to say goodbye. But it didn't matter how much vegetation I peeled off, the cracked stone kept its secrets, the dirt and grime of what could be centuries of wear obscuring the name.

A part of me wanted to go home and grab a scrub brush and some soap, the crazy thought there and gone in an instant. I didn't know the first thing about restoring an old headstone. I'd likely ruin the damn thing, anyway. Frustrated with myself, I stood, turning back to Dahlia's car, but as I did, a bitter wind whipped through the graveyard. It was almost icy, chilling the spring air enough to cause goose bumps to rise along the length of my arms.

But it wasn't just the chill on the air. A faint niggle at

the back of my brain screamed at me to go, get out, to leave this place and never come back. Quickly, I picked through the broken headstones and giant weeds, marching double-time to the Audi. In half a minute I had the car started and out of there, pointing toward home.

It was weird pulling up to my own house after the night I'd had. Weirder still? The place looked no worse for wear. The Night Watch house was filled with cracks and toppled statues, broken light fixtures and debris. My house appeared as if nothing had touched it—at least from the outside. But as much as I wanted to assess the damage, it wasn't like I had my keys or a cell phone, or fuck all, really. So instead of going inside, I pivoted on a heel and headed to J's house next door.

Granted, the clock on Dahlia's dash said it wasn't quite seven in the morning, but J had woken me in the dead of night about a zillion times before. It was payback time. Smiling, I balled a fist to give my very best cop knock when the door opened right in front of me, my arm still midair. *So much for that.* J's dark head and sharp pale gaze evaluated me for about half a second before he latched a hand on my wrist and yanked me inside.

"Where in the high holy fuck have you been?" As far as openers went, it left something to be desired.

I opened my mouth to respond but was met with a hand in my face.

"No. I get woken up from a blissful post-sex sleep to a goddamn earthquake. Your house almost broke in half, we couldn't find you, and then Cap calls me before I've even had my morning coffee to tell me you're leaving the force to go be some kind of Warden? What the fuck, Darby. What. The. Fuck?"

Again, I parted my lips to respond but was cut off.

"Jimmy fixed your stupid house by the way. Maybe you'll actually be able to sell it before you leave me high and dry and without a partner, you asshole."

Okay, so we were having this out now. "Are you going to let me tell you what happened?" I growled. "Or are you going to continue yelling at me for shit I could in no way control? Because I've had a long night and this shit isn't making the fucking thing any better."

J crossed his beefy arms and glared at me. I took that as my cue to begin. "First, I really appreciate ya'll fixing my house and for looking for me in the first place. As far as the earthquake itself, I don't remember much of it. What I do know is that touching that fucking note Essex left was a shit-*tastic* idea."

"You *touched* the note?" J growled, bristling like a pissed-off cat. "After Jimmy sealed that bag shut?"

Skirting past him, I headed for his coffee pot. "It

wasn't exactly voluntary." I pulled a couple of mugs from the cabinet and poured each of us a cup of Joe. "It was like I wasn't in control. I tried to stop, but I just couldn't."

J grumbled before retrieving the creamer and doctoring his own mug. He shoved it across the counter at me, and I did the same. "And?"

Rolling my eyes, I took a sip of the blissful brew, swallowing it down before I continued. "And I felt like I was dying—which I damn well was—Bishop took me to Azrael, Azrael took out the souls, and then..." At the thought of Azrael, the lump I'd thought had gone away returned, making it hard to say this next part. "Then he and Sloane went to the Underworld to release them. She came back. He didn't."

I hid my face in the mug, taking another sip. It went down like molasses, but it stopped me from crying again. I'd been doing far too much of that.

"Oh, honey. Is he—"

"Dead?" I supplied, shoving my grief down deep so it wouldn't touch me. I couldn't start crying again. I wouldn't survive it. "Yeah. And Sloane is the new Angel of Death. She caught Essex, too. Though, I did get to shoot him in the process. It was in the arm and not the head, but the bastard is slippery."

J spat out his coffee, the spray hitting my arm. "What?"

"Gross," I grumbled, snatching the tea towel from the oven door and wiping it off. "Like I said, some shit has happened. In the middle of the Underworld mess, the ABI broke in and tried to arrest us all, but Sloane made a deal for immunity. Now I'm 'Warden of Knoxville'—whatever the fuck that means. I just got the news like three seconds ago, and apparently, Cap already knows about it, so that's fun."

J winced before taking another sip of his coffee. "Umm... in more fun news, he's on his way here."

"Cap?" Captain David Stevens—better known as "Cap" or "Uncle Dave," who had been my father's best friend since they were in diapers. There hadn't been a major family holiday, poker night, moving day, or milestone in my life without this man in it. Still, that didn't mean he didn't have his secrets. Hell, before a few days ago, I hadn't known he was a damn werewolf.

So much for knowing a man.

"You know, I went to call your dad on you, too. Got all the way to letting the line ring before I remembered."

J had always had a habit of tattling on me to my dad. Since we were kids, if I started doing something dangerous or stupid, I could count on J to get my dad involved. The thought stung so much, I smacked my coffee mug on the counter and leveled J with the worst of my glares.

"What?" he said, shrugging. "Just because you're trying to bottle up all your feelings until you fucking explode doesn't mean I will. You aren't the only one who lost him, Darby. You aren't the only one who watched him die. You weren't the only one who was kidnapped and beaten and goddamn tortured. So if I want to mourn the man who was more of a dad to me than my own was, I fucking well will, okay?"

I was a horrible friend—a horrible person. The most awful woman to ever live.

"I'm sorry I've left you alone to deal with this," I whispered, my throat clogged with tears I was so desperately trying to keep in. "I'm sorry I made you worry and didn't tell you what was going on. I—"

J cut me off again, but this time he did it with a hug. I couldn't hold back anymore. It was the very reason why I had been avoiding the conversation and this kind of hug for days now. There was a power in J's hugs. They made you feel at home—safe and warm and in a cocoon of acceptance. If you had grief in your heart, there was no way to not cry in one of those hugs. It was like a law or something.

The pair of us sobbed, hanging onto each other for dear life, full of tears and snot, and hiccupping breaths.

We'd done this through every heartbreak—be it a silly crush or losing a loved one—and avoiding it was one of the dumber things I could add to the laundry list of stupid shit I'd done in the past week.

This was how Cap and Jimmy found us—sobbing in a heap on the floor of J's pristinely white kitchen.

9

"Jesus Christ. Who died now?" Cap griped, fists on his hips as he inspected the pile J and I made.

I couldn't help it, I started giggling at the utter absurdity of it all. Because someone had died, and that laugh was the only thing holding me together. Well, that and J.

"Azrael," I deadpanned when I got my giggles under control. "And Essex once he divulges all his knowledge to the ABI." I decided to leave off the fact that it had almost been me that had died, too. He didn't need to know that.

J and I sat shoulder to shoulder on his kitchen floor, teary-eyed and snot-nosed and complete messes.

Cap's eye twitched as he knelt to look me in the eyes.

"This have anything to do with the call I got from *August Theodore Davenport, III*?" Cap sneered. "And what kind of name is that, and why does he need to attach the 'the third' on there? Like I give a shit his parents were completely unoriginal and couldn't think up something better?"

"That'd be a 'yep' on all counts. It figures the pompous prick would call you. What an asshole."

Jimmy held out a box of tissues, and I took a handful to mop up the state of my face. "Why does it figure?"

"Because I figure he's getting pushback from the powers that be." That tracked. If the council—whoever the fuck they were—wanted me in the Warden position, I had a feeling they wanted it yesterday. It made total sense that the little bastard would try to torch the life I had to speed the process along.

I filled Cap and Jimmy in on what had transpired over the last several hours—leaving out the mind-blowing sex and the damn near dying parts. Neither of them needed to know about that.

"Warden?" Jimmy breathed. "I've heard of the position, but I'm more concerned about the council just shoving you into the role. I thought these things happened with a bit more finesse."

Cap snorted and shoved back to standing. "Nothing the council does is with finesse." He shook his head as he began to pace. "Something big must be happening if they are putting the pressure on the ABI."

That's what I'd assumed, too—that's why this next bit was going to hurt like hell.

"Because of all this—the Warden shit and all the rest —I think I might need to hand in my badge," I said, that last bit barely audible even to my own ears.

"What?" All three men had said this at once, and I cringed.

But what else was I supposed to do? Remain a cop and work both sides of the fence? Try to solve cases in the human world in my free time? Who knew what else I'd be doing?

I tossed my hands up, wad of tissues in my fists and all. "You got a better idea? I was under the impression the position was nonnegotiable. You want me to stay a cop and do whatever this job is?"

It was too much. Too much pressure, too much uncertainty.

Cap sighed, stopping his pacing to shoot me with a look that said he was offended. "No. I want you to be smart about this and not just hand in your papers because some asshole in a suit told you to. I can put you on leave indefinitely. That way you're still on the force. If this shit goes sideways, I want you to be able to come back home if you need to."

J snorted. "You just want to delay the inevitable. Darby was never meant to stay in this town, Cap. We all know that."

I slid to the side to give my best friend my full attention. "What's that supposed to mean?"

"Exactly what I said," J shot back. "How many cases have you solved in Knoxville or Ascension? How many arcaners have you helped that had nothing to do with this town? It sounds like you've been doing the job for years—you just weren't getting paid."

Grumbling, I crossed my arms over my chest—yes, like a pouty toddler. "But I want to stay here."

"Weren't you the one just saying you needed to quit?" Jimmy asked, his voice kind even though his words called me all the way out. "Which is it? You staying, or are you going?"

I wanted to kick my feet and pound my fists into the ground. I didn't—I wasn't that much of a child—but damn if I didn't want to. "I don't know, okay? I want J as my partner. I want you taking pictures. I want to slide into Cap's office and eat my sandwich as we razz each other over the poker game he lost the night before. I want to see the ghosts I normally see every day at the station. I want my house. I want my dad. I want to be safe and not worry everyone I love is going to be a target. But I want to help people, and more and more the arcane side is coming into this side of my life, and I keep putting you all in danger."

"You mean me," J whispered, bumping his big shoulder against mine. "Cap and Jimmy are already in this world with you."

I balled the tissues in my hand and got up, throwing them in the trash. I didn't want to confirm J's assumption. "I want the people in my life to be safe, J. You are in my life. You're my best friend. Put the shoe on the other foot, and I got beaten up and kidnapped and damn near killed by shit you were in the middle of. Would you want to stick around me, knowing it could happen again?"

"That's not fair," J growled, hauling himself to standing.

"It never is," I answered, echoing Dahlia's earlier words. She'd been so right. None of this was even in the realm of fair.

"So, you're just going to cut me out? Stick me in a box and put me away because it's convenient for you?"

I wanted to bring up all the times he'd done the same thing to me. When he'd pretended I couldn't talk to ghosts at all because it creeped him out or made me look like a loon. When he wouldn't even let me talk to Hildy in front of him because he was afraid. I had to clench my jaw so tight to not let that out, I was afraid I might have broken my teeth.

"None of this is convenient, and you pulling that shit isn't, either. I don't want to put you in a box. I want you to not get kidnapped and damn near beaten to death."

Did I mean to shout that last bit? No.

Did I? Abso-fucking-lutely.

J took a step back, his face ashen. "I know I didn't always have your back before. I know I fucked up, but don't cut me out now. I'm in this, okay?" He broke our stare and shifted his gaze to Jimmy. "I'm in this, and I'm not leaving, so everyone just needs to get used to it."

I got the impression J and Jimmy had had this discussion more than once over the last few days.

Jimmy held his hands up in surrender. "I didn't say anything."

"Your face said it for you."

Jimmy's cheeks went red, and the giant Viking of a man clenched his jaw. "How about you fucking run when I tell you to run, dammit, and I won't have that look on my face."

J blinked back tears. "They were beating you," he whispered. "Cut your hair and your ears. They—"

"I know what they did," Jimmy hissed. "But you could have gotten away. You wouldn't have been hurt. Cap was holding them off. Yeah, they already had

Killian, but you could have run, and you didn't. Instead, you got beat right alongside me. Cut my hair, take my ears, whatever. Watching them hurt you was worse than all that."

It made me sick when I'd seen what had happened to J and Jimmy—the images had whirled in their brains as their pain had threatened to pull me under. I supposed that was one perk to not hearing everyone's thoughts anymore, though it seemed like a poor victory.

"And you," Jimmy barked, staring right at me. "If I hear about one more martyrdom bullshit, I will personally kick your ass. It doesn't matter whatever weird magic your father gave you." He waved his hand at me, encompassing all that I was. "No more of this sacrificing yourself crap. That's done, you hear me?"

I thought back to all the times I'd been forced to choose someone else over myself, forced to weigh whether or not I wanted someone to die because of me. There were only a handful of people in my life that I would do that for, and three of them were in this room. If any one of them were on the chopping block, I wouldn't hesitate to offer myself instead. "Yeah, Jimmy. I'll get right on that."

"You're a pain in my ass, you know that?" Cap growled. "And it pisses me off that I'm still here and your dad isn't. It pisses me off that the council thinks they can just whisk you off to Knoxville right underneath me. And you know what else?"

I couldn't help the slight pull to my lips because Uncle Dave going on a rant was so rare it was a sight to behold. "What?"

"You being Warden is actually a good thing, and it makes me mad enough to spit because you'll do a great job. So great, you won't want to come home anymore."

"No one said I had to *live* there." I scoffed. "I have a perfectly good house just sitting right there." I gestured in the direction of where my average-sized three-bedroom sat.

It was a cute little home, if a bit smaller than I'd like. It had wooden shudders and a darling little yard that I mowed myself when I had the time. When I didn't, Dad would come over and mow it for me. Hell, we even planted the zinnias in the flower bed last spring, the multicolored blooms giving a pop of color to the rather bland neighborhood.

There wasn't an inch of that house that didn't have a memory stamped on it.

"I'm not going anywhere. I'm just taking a different job is all. We'll still have poker nights and Monster Mash Movie Mondays in October and all the other shit. None of that is changing."

Not if I could help it, anyway.

Dave wrapped me up in a hug so reminiscent of my father's I thought I was going to die inside. "It better not, kid. I expect full participation in all major family holidays and functions. And I get final approval over this ABI agent you've been courting. I don't want to fall down on the job."

I snickered. "He won't be an ABI agent for very much longer. He's quitting."

Dave pulled back. "Really?"

Chuckling, I nodded. "He asked if I needed a deputy or something." A smile stretched across my face. "At least one thing is going right."

I knew I shouldn't have said it. It was like I was purposefully flipping off Fate, or just begging for the world to come smack me down. As soon as the words left my mouth, Hildy appeared right next to me, making me jump right out of Uncle Dave's arms.

"Jesus H. Christ, Hildy. You scare—"

"Tell everyone to get down. Right now," he shouted. "There are witches co—"

But he didn't get to finish that sentence before the world went white as all the windows in J's living room blew in.

10

Ringing drowned out every sound as I tried to pick myself up off the floor. Flickers of orange light danced over everything, the heat of the fire next door seeping into my skin. Hildy was yelling in my face, but whatever sense that let me hear his ghostly voice seemed to be knocked out as well. I scanned J's living room, my gaze landing on J and Jimmy first before finding Uncle Dave.

J was easy to locate, he was under Jimmy, the Viking-sized elf covering him with his whole body. Blood bloomed over the shoulder of Jimmy's white shirt as small glass shards protruded from the cloth like glittering spikes. A hand filled my field of vision, and I grabbed it, allowing Uncle Dave to haul me to my feet. He had blood on his face but no wounds, the werewolf healing process working far faster than I thought it would. I avoided looking down at myself, the stinging ache in my cheek, hand, and arm telling the tale far better than my eyes could.

The world might have spun as soon as I was pulled upright, but I got a front-row seat to Dave's wolfy rage— a sight I'd never seen before. His eyes glowed amber, his canines growing into fangs before he seemed to gather his control. Then all of a sudden, the sound was turned back on.

Hildy got in between Dave and I, his cold, ghostly touch snapping me out of my daze. "Tell them it was the witches, lass. Jesus, Mary, and Joseph, lass. I need you to look at me, read my lips or something."

"I can hear you," I croaked, fighting off the urge to inspect the burning ache in my arm. "Witches?"

Hildy sagged a little bit before shooting me a hard look. "I told ya there would be consequences for ya disbanding that coven." He gestured to the orange light that flickered in the direction of my house. "Exhibit A."

Shoving away my initial thoughts about the state of my home, I settled on justified rage instead. I'd had a damn good reason to disband the Knoxville Coven. One, they'd tried to open a hole in the fucking fabric of reality so they would have a direct line to the power of the Underworld. Two, the majority of them *had not* been under mind control when they'd decided on this course of action. And three? They killed my dad. The fact that I wasn't hunting them down one by one and putting a bullet in their brains was a goddamn gift.

One I planned on taking back at the very first opportunity.

"They fucking well started it. I didn't threaten to unmake the world, now, did I? No." Though when I'd disbanded said coven, I might have been a little more juiced up than I was right then—a fact I did not want to advertise at all. It was one thing to disband a coven when you had thousands of souls' worth of power backing you up.

It was quite another to be human strength with a penchant for talking to ghosts.

"We can hash this out later. Get a weapon or somethin'. They're still out there. Ya might be able to catch them if ya quit yapping your gums about right and wrong."

I fought off rolling my eyes at him and translated. Without so much as a peep, Uncle Dave slapped his ankle piece in my hand. It was small, the lightweight pistol fitting in my palm quite nicely. Dave gestured for us to follow, leading the lot of us out of J's back door and into the yard. J trailed behind me, but Jimmy was nowhere to be seen, the glint of a sword catching my eye for a split second before it was gone. I didn't know where Jimmy had gone, but I'd seen firsthand the Fae pop in out of nowhere.

J tapped my back three times, signaling that he was okay and behind me. It was an old code we'd used about a zillion times as kids. Granted when we were children it hadn't been because we were stalking witches, but whatever. The spring morning air had a faint chill to it despite the blaze, the wind carrying the stench of burning wood and spent magic.

The air shimmered for a second, and then Dave was no longer in front of me. Or rather he was, but in a different form. Where a very tall man had once stood was now a sleek gray wolf, his coat gleaming in the dawning sun and dancing firelight. He tilted his head back, sniffing the air before he huffed once and turned. Picking through the side yard, he led us toward the front of J's house, the six-foot privacy fence our only cover against discovery.

Hildy's grayed-out visage popped out of the side gate, half his body still on the other side. "There's only two of them, but the way they're talking, they don't have the first clue about exacting revenge. We need to nip this shite in the bud while we can. And tell your pup to turn back, we'll have company soon enough."

Two voices shouted over the sound of the flames. At

first, I thought it was another incantation, but it only took about another second to figure out that they were arguing.

"You were supposed to blow up the whole house, you moron," one of them screeched. "Not just the living room. How are we supposed to know if we got her if you don't demolish the whole thing?"

J shoved forward and silently unlatched the gate. All three of us peeked through the sliver in the opening. Two women stood in broad daylight staring at the ruin of my house. One a blunt-bobbed brunette in an Oxford shirt and flats, and the other a slender lime-haired Stevie Nicks wannabe, complete with fringed shawl, broomstick skirt, and rings on every finger.

The ringed woman shoved the preppy one hard enough to make her stumble. "You were supposed to tell me what room she was in. You pointed to the front window, so that's the one I blasted. It's not rocket science."

I glanced down and away to keep from laughing. Like, was this what I was up against? Two idiot witches who couldn't do something so basic as a locator spell to check if I was home or not? Dave's wolfy head tilted back to peer at me, giving me a look that said, "What do you want to do?"

Shrugging, I shifted my gaze back to the witches who

continued to bicker and shove at each other. I knew I'd said I'd kill all Knoxville witches on sight, but the thought of taking out these two just seemed wrong. Not to mention, I didn't recall these two being up at the lake. No, if I had a guess the pair had to be wannabes or hired guns. Though, I hoped whoever had paid these two idiots got their money back.

My shrug must have given Dave carte blanche because he snaked around the side of the gate and let loose a growl that made even me freeze. Then I got my ass in gear, following the giant wolf as I lifted my weapon. I felt more than saw J at my back, the three of us carefully stepping across the charred lawn.

It took a few seconds before the two idiots registered Uncle Dave, and even longer to gather the wherewithal to understand that not only had they not killed me, but they were as close to screwed as they could possibly be. Then in the next instant, Jimmy appeared, his sword drawn like he was ready to take their heads.

At the first flicker of magic, Dave's growl got practically demonic. The low rumble of sound vibrated through my chest like a damn drum, and they finally got smart—well, smart enough for them, anyway.

Honestly, I couldn't even keep my gun on them. "This is just embarrassing."

The lime-haired one sneered at me. "What's

embarrassing is you thinking you could just disband us without repercussions."

Both J and I snorted. "Is 'repercussions' you *not* killing me, because I'm not seeing it. Ya'll getting low on actual thinkers in that coven of yours or what? You couldn't do a locator spell to figure out I wasn't in that house? I thought that was Witchy Woo-Woo 101."

The preppy brunette scowled, crossing her arms over her chest. "We got close, didn't we?"

The air shimmered for a moment before Dave stood on two feet. "Anyone ever tell you close only counts in horseshoes and hand grenades?"

Both ladies stepped back, not bothering to try and toss a spell at him.

All I could do was just blink at them, appalled. Shiloh would have had their asses. The former Knoxville coven leader was fastidious and thorough. No way would she have accepted this level of sloppy. "I know you weren't trained by Shiloh St. James because you don't have the first fucking clue, and I know you weren't up at that lake because I know the name of every witch who was there, and I don't know you two. What? Did everyone with a brain just leave ya'll behind? Or were you even a member of the Knoxville Coven? Because I don't see it."

The Stevie wannabe flinched like I'd slapped her, and

Preppy appeared a little green around the gills. Being this close to them, I got a better sense of their ages, pegging them closer to late teens rather than the early twenties as I'd originally thought. Yeah, killing them wouldn't be on the table. Though, the ABI would want them for questioning.

Sucks to be them.

"You weren't members, were you? Too young, maybe? Not enough training."

Stevie shot Preppy an expression of pure fear, and I understood. These weren't Knoxville witches. These two were outcasts. Misfits. And in no way had this shit been their idea.

"Someone put you up to this."

Hildy popped into view, nearly startling me out of my inspection of the witches. "I believe you said you'd kill Knoxville witches on sight. What are ya waiting for?"

I gave him the ultimate side-eye. "They are actual children. I'm not killing kids, Hildy, and if these girls are over the age of eighteen, I'll eat my hat."

Hell, I couldn't even point my gun at them and passed off the weapon to Dave, who seemed to be thinking the same damn thing I was. The only people who actually stayed on task were J and Jimmy, but even Jim appeared ready to drop his sword.

"Who are you talking to?" a snotty voice asked, and I

couldn't tell if it was Stevie or Preppy, so I answered them both.

"I'm a grave talker, you idiots. There are ghosts just about everywhere, and what do grave talkers do?" At their blank stares, I answered my own question, "We talk to them."

Staring up at the brightening sky, I hoped the ABI could straighten these girls out before they learned enough to hurt themselves.

"What the fuck?" a familiar voice barked.

I moved my eyes, if not my head, to stare at Bishop. Unlike me, he'd picked up shoes at some point, his booted feet crunching across my charred grass as he emerged from the waning shadows. His black T-shirt stretched across his broad chest, accentuating the gear clipped to his belt. A long lock of hair fell across his forehead, giving his savage expression just a little more *oomph.*

I really should not be turned on right now. But I was—I *so* was.

Before I could answer him, sirens pealed through the air, the distinct wails of police and fire engines.

"Please tell me you have handcuffs," I said by way of greeting.

Gold light filled his irises as his gaze locked on the two witches. "Considering I haven't had the time to turn in my badge yet? Absolutely."

Bishop pulled out a set of cuffs and unerringly hooked up Stevie before catching another pair from J and giving Preppy the same treatment. Around the time he got them properly secured, the fire engine screamed down my street, a pair of black-and-whites arriving right behind them.

This was going to be a long day.

11

"I should have killed those little bitches when I had the chance," I muttered as I inspected what was left of my living room. My favorite chair—the cerulean one with the crushed velvet upholstery was dead. It wasn't just dead. It was burnt to a crisp, broken in four pieces, and half-melted in some places.

I didn't even want to go into what had happened to my coffee pot.

"I thought you said that you couldn't kill children," Hildy reminded me, and I'd never wanted to stab a ghost as much as I did right then. "Are you a murderer or not, lass? I forget in my old age."

"Oh, fuck you, Hildenbrand."

After the firemen put out my house and the police

carted off the witches—Bishop assured me the ABI would be meeting them at the station to take custody— I'd been allowed to enter the smoking remains of what had been a rather nice living room. I'd chosen each piece myself, mixing stuff from antique shops and big box stores and making it my own. Yes, most of the place was still intact, but I'd need to completely remodel the living room and kitchen if I actually wanted to be able to live here.

Luckily, the fire hadn't spread to the bedrooms, so I had my books and clothes, but it still sucked.

J nudged me with his shoulder, and I glanced up from my chair-mourning. A decked-out fireman named Shultz was staring at me like I was completely bonkers. I really needed to stop talking to Hildy in public.

Shooting the man a sheepish wave, I said, "What? You don't name your chairs?"

That bonkers look did not get any better. Maybe I should just stop talking altogether.

Bishop patted him on the shoulder. "I think we've got it under control here. We promise not to go near any of the structures you've indicated are dangerous."

"Yeah, Shultzy, we'll take it from here," J echoed, guiding the guy out of my ruin of a house.

I shot an irritated glare at Hildy. "Could you fucking

not?" I hissed. "It's bad enough I have to deal with this shit. Stop piling on me just because you think it's funny."

Hildy flickered a bit, becoming solid for a second before he faded back to his usual gray. "You can't paint a target on your back and then just let people go, lass. Letting the coppers take those girls was a mistake, and you know it."

Yes, I'd totally just said I should have killed them, but I hadn't meant it. Not really, anyway. "Would you have?"

"I wouldn't have painted the target to begin with."

"Bullshit," I hissed. "This coming from the man who waged wars and fought legions? You've painted plenty of targets in your day, Hildy. Don't rewrite history to teach me a lesson. They were kids. Anyone with half a brain could see that, and I wasn't going to turn myself into a monster just to save my own skin."

A smile bloomed over Hildy's face. "That's my girl."

I wanted to smile back, but a flicker of hurt ignited in my chest. This was a thing he and I did—he'd test me to see if I would do something shitty, always surprised when I didn't choose myself over someone else. It took a long time to get it, but now that I did, I hated every single memory of one of his tests. Because they had never been about me—they had always been about Mariana.

"I'm not her," I whispered. "I've never been her. You don't need to keep testing me."

My mother—his daughter—had been an evil, conniving, manipulative she-beast of a woman. But she hadn't raised me.

Killian had. Hell, the nicest thing she'd ever done for me was leaving me behind.

Bishop tossed an arm over my shoulder, reeling me into his side. His jaw clenched like he'd really enjoy giving Hildy a piece of his mind, but his lips stayed shut. I let his warmth seep into me as he guided me through the tattered, smoking remnants of my living room to the bedroom.

I did need to gather some clothes, even though most of them would smell like smoke.

"I know you aren't her, lass. It's just... I failed as a father with her. The lessons I taught her didn't stick and—"

That had my feet stopping all on their own. "You didn't fail her. Mariana made her own choices—her own way. She chose to be the way she was, chose to not see that she had everything she wanted. A family. Power. A name for herself. She chose to hurt people, to kill. That's on her. Not you." I paused, wiping a stupid tear off my face. "And I am not—nor have I ever been—Mariana O'Shea."

Without another word, I plowed forward, heading right for my closet and the closest suitcase. It was a hard-sided thing I'd taken with me to college. Dad had gotten it for me, telling me I should have proper luggage if I was going to be an adult. Sure, U of T was only an hour from home, but he'd wanted me to have the full college experience—dorm rooms and all.

Packing took less time than I thought—especially since Bishop snagged a weekender bag from the shelf and started filling it up with weapons, arcane books, and the like. I'd gathered the last of my toiletries when the besuited Davenport plowed through my ruined house, his blond hair out of sorts.

Hildy followed him into the room, eyeing the ABI director with a solid level of contempt.

Cheeks red and tie skewed, he opened his mouth and put his foot right in it. "I thought I told you—"

"Nope," I said, cutting him off. "See here, what we're not going to do is have you coming in here thinking I'm the sibling to be messed with." I ripped the zipper on the bag shut. I knew Sloane had kept my name out of her mouth on purpose, but there was no way this asshole didn't know who my parents were. No. Way. "I know you're just trying to cover your own ass with the council, but don't for one second think I won't sick Hildy on you to make sure you never sleep again. I might not be Death herself, but don't test me."

Hildy, to his credit, backed me up, turning himself solid for a second—just long enough to whisper "Boo" right in Davenport's face before winking back out of sight.

The director skittered a few steps, slamming himself against the wall. Inside I was laughing my ass off, but outside? My face was smooth as granite as I gave the director a bored stare.

"Now, you were saying?"

Davenport traced a shaking hand over his haphazard tie as he attempted to gather himself. "Party tricks will only work for so long, you know."

"I know." I shrugged, pulling my suitcase from the bed. "Then I'll have to get creative. Do you want to find out how creative I can be?"

Sloane had said he was a murderer, right? I wondered how many of those souls took their secrets to their graves, and how many would be willing to share said secrets. I could get very creative if the need arose.

Davenport's face paled. "I think we got off on the wrong foot." He raked a hand through his windswept hair, putting himself back to rights. "What I meant to say was that I would appreciate it if you allowed me to escort you to the Warden house in Knoxville. It has far better security than your home at the current moment, and you would be safer there."

I hated that he was right. Those two witches may not be the only ones out there, and I'd feel a hell of a lot better if I wasn't painting a target on my friends' backs. That didn't mean I had to tell him that.

"And it would get the council off your back. Having me installed in the Warden house makes it look like you've done your job, correct?"

The small man sighed hard enough, the threat of his soul escaping the confines of his body was a real possibility. "Correct. The—"

"Okay," I replied, cutting off whatever bullshit diatribe he was about to let fall out of his mouth.

"Okay?" Both Bishop and Davenport said at the same time.

I raised my eyebrows at the two men. "What? My house has a hole in it for fuck's sake. It's not like I have a ton of options—especially since I'm taking the job. Might as well get this over with."

Davenport's eyes narrowed. "Too easy. No daughter of Mariana O'Shea would give in just like that."

Way wrong thing to say.

"Mariana O'Shea did not raise me. Killian Adler did. And you saying that I'm nothing like her is a fucking compliment." I winced, looking at Hildy. "No offense."

"None taken, lass."

Bishop stepped around me, putting himself between me and the director. "Maybe don't throw around the 'Mom' card on this one? We're all trying to be friends here, aren't we?"

"And what stake do you have in it, La Roux? Shouldn't you have turned your paperwork in already?"

Bishop let out a dark chuckle that had all the hair on my arms raising at once but didn't answer him. Instead, he hefted the weapons bag on his shoulder and snagged my rolling suitcase. Then he held out his hand for mine, and I took it, letting him lead me past Davenport and out of the house.

I didn't know what beef Bishop and the director had, but I sure as hell didn't want to be Davenport when Bishop wasn't a member of the ABI anymore. Davenport must have realized this, too, because he changed the subject as he followed us out.

He held up a business card in between two fingers. "The address to the Warden house. I'll meet you there—make sure you're settled in."

Not only did I not want to take the card—I was

pretty sure I would have PTSD from touching any form of cardstock for the rest of my days—the thought of having Davenport "settling me in" made my skin crawl. I stared at the card, not making any move to take it.

"I know where it is," Bishop answered. "We'll see you there."

Davenport sniffed, tucking the card back in his breast pocket. "So be it. I expect your resignation papers on my desk before the end of the day, La Roux."

Bishop let go of my hand and pulled the badge from his belt. "Why wait?" He tossed it to the director before pulling a sheaf of folded papers from his back pocket. Davenport fumbled with the badge for a second before managing to catch it. "These have already been signed off by HR, so you're saving me a trip."

Bishop slapped the folded papers against Davenport's chest, holding them there until the shocked man took them.

"Five centuries with us and you're just going to throw it all away?" The director seemed aghast, as if he couldn't fathom why Bishop would toss out all that time.

"Why would I want to be released from what amounted to indentured servitude, you mean? Gee. Let me think." Bishop grabbed my hand again. "I never had a choice whether I wanted to work for you or not. It was *you* that kept me there, threatening termination every time I so much as stepped a toe out of line."

Davenport took a step back. "Not me. I trusted O'Shea and Drake to do their jobs. What else did they do?"

"Maybe you should ask your Overseer." Bishop sneered. "And in the future? Maybe look in on your staff once in a while. Make sure they're actually doing their jobs instead of executing a centuries-long vendetta that sullies the ABI's name. Just a thought."

With that, Bishop led the way to my Jeep and pressed the key fob, unlocking the doors. Somehow, neither my nor Dahlia's car had been damaged in the blast. Either that, or Jimmy must have worked his mojo before I noticed. I took my keys from him, and Bishop tossed the bags in the back, the pair of us ignoring Davenport with the best of our ability.

"I think I'll be following him if you don't mind, lass," Hildy said from my back seat. "See what I can glean before he heads back to his office. Stupid warding."

I hummed my agreement, careful not to change my expression as I started the Jeep.

"And I'll be looking into who sent those witches. If that's the best the Knoxville coven's got, I'll eat my cane."

Smiling, I gave the director a finger wave through the windshield. Humming once more, I gave Hildy a slight nod.

Davenport was going to have a shadow for the foreseeable future.

12

As soon as Davenport got the hint and left, I immediately turned the Jeep off and got back out, heading straight for a small huddle of men. J, Jimmy, and Dave stood off to the side of my house, having a quiet conversation with my other neighbor, Mr. Thurgood.

Oliver Thurgood lived on the other side of me, closer to the park, and I had to wonder if his house had taken damage as well. He was a small older man who likely bought in the neighborhood because he thought it was going to be quiet.

Oops.

"I saw those girls sneaking around the property and called the police. I know you two are the police, too, but I didn't know if ya'll needed backup or not. Plus, Ms.

Adler has been through enough with her father dying and all."

Placing a gentle hand on Mr. Thurgood's shoulder, I shot him a grateful smile. "I really appreciate that. Thank you. I'm so sorry for the trouble. Was your house damaged at all?"

Mr. Thurgood covered my hand with his weathered one, a sense of peace hitting me at his papery touch. "Oh, no. My house is fine. Just a little singed grass, but that'll come back. I think most of the damage was farther south, closer to Cooper's property."

Mr. Thurgood was one of the few people on the street that didn't look at me like I was a circus performer. A small crowd still gathered on the park side of the street on the sidewalk, hissing like snakes as they gave me, my house, and the whole tableau disapproving looks.

Well, excuse me. It isn't like I blew my house up all by myself.

"I'll supervise these young men boarding up your window, too. That way you can go get some rest. What, with the funeral and the earthquake and now this, you must be exhausted. Shoot, I've lived in Tennessee my whole life and never felt an earthquake like that."

Earthquakes weren't unheard of in this part of Tennessee. This close to a fault line, we got tremors every once in a while. But whatever I'd done had apparently shaken the whole damn neighborhood.

"That is so kind of you to say, Mr. Thurgood."

"I have told you for three years straight to call me Oliver."

There was no way on this green earth that I would ever in a million years call Mr. Thurgood Oliver. I smiled at him. "Of course."

Bishop's approach rattled through my senses, and I looked up just in time to see the gold flash in his irises. "Take your hand off of her. Now."

Mr. Thurgood's hand flew off of mine, and I drew my fingers away from his shoulder. "I didn't mean anything by it. She was just so—"

"I don't care. Don't touch her again," Bishop growled, wrapping an arm around my middle and attempting to draw me away.

I elbowed him in the stomach and whirled on him, getting in between him and my neighbor. "What the hell is your problem? Mr. Thurgood has been nothing but sweet to me the entire time I've lived here. I don't kno—"

"He's an incubus," Bishop hissed, and the whole group went wired. Or well, J and Dave did, but Jimmy just stood there like this wasn't exactly new information. "Or he's mixed with one. He was stealing emotions from you." Bishop skirted around me and stared Mr. Thurgood down with a vehemence that spoke of the utmost violence.

Was Haunted Peak really Monster Central and no one told me? I had been under the impression there weren't any arcaners in this town, but the more I hung around Bishop, the more I realized that this just wasn't true.

"I am *not* an incubus," Mr. Thurgood said. "I'm a mara—we're different. For one, I'm not a damn demon, and for two, I just sip the negativity off people I care about. And if I want to take some anxiety and fear from a friend, I damn well will. Can't you see how much darkness is in her? Can't you see how much she's hurting? You think I don't know what she did for us? She deserves respect and not hate like those fools over there." He nodded toward the group of gossiping onlookers.

I took a giant step back from the group as a whole. "I'm sorry, *what?*"

"I didn't mean any harm—" he began, but I cut him off with a raised hand, pinning my eyes on J.

"Are you and your mom the only freaking humans in this town, or what?"

J shrugged, his wide eyes pinned on our neighbor. "I'm starting to think so."

Mr. Thurgood chuckled. "There are plenty of humans

in this town, child. It's just that Haunted Peak isn't like other places."

But he didn't elaborate, and I didn't ask. Instead, Bishop scolded what had to be an eighty-five-year-old man. "This isn't like the old days. In this day and age, you need to ask someone before you take emotions. Haven't you heard of consent? If you don't want to be called an incubus, don't act like one."

Mr. Thurgood stepped back like Bishop had socked him in the gut. "Fair enough, young man." Then he turned to me. "I apologize for taking without asking. I will from now on."

Not knowing how else to respond—because it wasn't every day that you found out your neighbor was stealing emotions from you—I just nodded, wide-eyed, and passed my keys to Bishop. "We better get going before Davenport comes back and frog-marches me to Knoxville."

We said our goodbyes to J, Jimmy, and Dave as Mr. Thurgood toddled off, his shoulders drooping. I didn't know how to feel about all the new information I'd just received, but the sight made my heart hurt.

"You're going to make sure these guys do a good job, right?" I called to his back, and the elderly man perked up, tossing me a shy smile. He might have gone about it the wrong way, but I knew a friend when I saw one. Mr.

Thurgood had been one of the few people in town to not treat me like a freak, and I wasn't going to burn that bridge unless I damn well had to.

"Will do, Darby. And I'll keep an eye out for anyone else, too." He paused, frowning. "If that's okay with you?"

I knew I could count on Oliver Thurgood. "That would be very helpful, thank you."

Mr. Thurgood shot me a beaming smile, his eyes flashing electric green for a second before fading back to a watery blue. Yep, I'd done the right thing for once.

By the time Bishop and I made it to Knoxville, I was dead on my feet. I actually couldn't remember the last time I'd slept. Was it two or three days ago that I put my father in the ground?

Maybe it was one day, I couldn't actually recall.

The so-called Warden house was a sprawling, gray Victorian, with an honest-to-god turret. Davenport stood on the porch, glaring at us as we peeled ourselves from the Jeep. My feet felt like they'd been encased in lead blocks, and even though Bishop had gotten me a coffee bigger than my head, I still could barely keep my eyes open. The porch steps were more akin to Mount Everest than a set of stairs.

"About time you two got here," Davenport griped. "I am a busy man, Adler. We have cases to go over, agents to meet, and the—"

I shook my head, praying I stayed upright. "No."

"What do you mean, 'no'? If you plan—"

"No," I repeated, hauling myself up the steps by sheer force of will. "I am going to sleep. After I'm rested, I will gladly look over the cases on my docket. I might get to the other things, too, but sleep is paramount."

Growling, Davenport turned his back to me, and Bishop and I followed him inside. The entryway was a gorgeous assortment of old-world details and contemporary charm. Granted, there was also a hideous floral wallpaper, but the moldings appeared original and the space clean. The director marched through the entryway and deeper into the house, leading us to a modern kitchen that had three men sitting at the giant island with a mess of case files spread out over every surface.

Well, three men and a ghost, but I chose not to acknowledge the nearly see-through boy standing next to the island—especially since I didn't know who he belonged to.

All three agents looked up when Davenport entered as if they were sitting at attention, while the ghost floated away from the angry director as if he feared him.

"These are the agents assigned to you. Agents Yazzie, Acker, and Tobin. They will assist you on cases until you can build your staff." When I opened my mouth to argue, he plowed forward. "Don't start. The council told me I had to help with the transition, so that's what I'm doing. You want to argue, do it with them."

Sheepish, one of the agents stood, holding out a hand to shake. He was tall, maybe six feet two or three, with deep golden skin and amber eyes. His black hair fell in a sheet down his back, and the sharpness to his features appeared to lend toward Native American or First Nations heritage.

"Jensen Yazzie, ma'am. Nice to meet you," he murmured in a soft voice, instantly putting me at ease.

"Darby Adler," I replied, taking his hand. "It's very nice to meet you, too."

The other two agents kept their seats. The first a tow-headed meathead with a red face and odd red-brown eyes. He didn't introduce himself, and it was obvious he in no way wanted to be here. The second shot the angry agent a frightened expression before shakily standing and offering his pale hand for me to shake.

"Aldrich Tobin," the agent announced, shaking my hand with a tenuous grip. He was exceptionally tall, but stood hunched as if he was trying to make himself smaller. His features were a shade past gaunt, and it made me want to feed him until he couldn't eat any more.

"I-I do tech and surveillance work. Umm... that is if you want to keep me. I know you can dismiss us if you want to. A-Acker here specializes in curses and counter-curses and blood bonds. Yazzie does all the were and shifter stuff. Customs, courtesies, and whatnot. We had another agent who specialized in mage workings, but since the boss said La Roux was coming, she left. Umm... do you want coffee, 'cause I can get yo—"

"That's enough, Tobin," Davenport snarled, tossing an irritated hand through his blond hair. "As Agent Tobin informed you, each agent has been selected based on their skill set. They will reside here with you and La Roux until you can choose a team of your own. They are on loan only so don't get attached. I fully intend on taking them back. Now, if you insist on delaying your orientation, I will be off. I suggest you sleep fast. I have no intention of letting the council breathe down my neck just so you can get your beauty rest."

Rather than get into it with Davenport in front of his subordinates, I simply stared at the director until he got the hint. Growling, the small man spun on his loafer and left, slamming right back out the front door.

With Davenport gone, the ghost boy floated closer,

inspecting me. He was tow-headed and pale, with pretty dark eyes and an innocent face.

Exhaustion hit me hard, and I pulled off my messenger bag, dumping it on the kitchen table and jerking out a chair. There was no way I was going to be able to sleep with a loose ghost in the house. Hildy was one thing, but kid ghosts were quite another.

"Tobin, I would love coffee if you would be so kind. As a general house rule, there should probably always be a pot brewed." He hopped up, racing toward the coffee maker so fast, I thought he was going to hurt himself. I assessed Acker—his expression hadn't changed a single millimeter since I'd walked in. "Also, as a general house rule, I don't allow untethered ghosts in the house, so which one of ya'll had a young tow-headed family member who died at about seven years old?"

The boy raced for me, his face getting right in front of mine so fast it nearly made me fall out of my seat. "You can see me? I can't believe it. Can you tell my brother something for me? I won't ask anything else, I swear."

I held up a hand as I pinched my brow. "Slow down, kid. I'll tell him, but you gotta back up. You get too close to me and it's a one-way ticket to the Underworld."

The boy backed up, sheepish, and turned to stare at

the angry agent. Acker went from just red-faced to looking ready to spit nails.

Ding, ding, ding. We have a winner.

"What's your name, kid?" I asked, summarily ignoring Acker. If he wanted to hate me, fine, but I was getting this ghost out of the house. Probably him, too, if he didn't cool it.

"Linus. Ambrose is my brother—twin actually. Can you tell him that it was my fault? That I'm sorry."

I stared at the child for a moment before shifting my gaze to his twin. Linus' clothing was from the early 1900s, but Ambrose didn't appear older than twenty at a push. It had me wondering what brand of arcaner he was, though the curses specialty made me think sorcerer or warlock.

Did I want to get in the middle of family drama? No. But kid ghosts required a bit of finesse.

I relayed the message, and got an incredibly pissed-off man in my face for my trouble. "He didn't say that. You're just making it up to scare me, you bitch."

Now, there were two ways I could go about this. I could let Bishop lose his shit—which I figured was about to happen any second now, considering I could see swirls of black and purple out of the corner of my eye—or I could show Acker that trying to use his size to intimidate me was a bad plan.

I went with door number two.

Men like Acker always left their gut open, expecting a sock to the jaw before they ever thought of one to the solar plexus. My jab had him doubled over, and then it was just a matter of my knee in his nose, and he was laid out on the kitchen floor. Blood poured from his now-broken nose, and the big man tried to stem the flow as he curled in a ball on the ground.

"Two things," I murmured as I knelt next to him, my voice nice and calm so he understood that I was dead serious. "One, I don't lie as a habit, but I especially do not lie about ghosts. I would never relay a message that a specter did not want me to send. I might not always tell you when they are here or everything they say, but I don't put words in their mouths. And two?"

Acker's reddish eyes speared me with a glare of pure hate, but I sallied forth. "Because this had to do with family, I will let this little outburst go with a warning. But if you ever use your size or power to try and intimidate me again, it will be the last fucking thing you do. Understand?"

I didn't expect an answer, so I returned my gaze to his brother. "Tell me something only you and he would know."

Linus went on to tell me about the time they went swimming at the pond by their farm. They didn't want to get their clothes wet, so they went in naked, and Ambrose got a leech stuck on his—

"Whoa. TMI, little dude." I shuddered before spearing Ambrose with an evil smile. "I just heard about the leech incident. Tell me—do you still have a scar on your business?" I snickered, gesturing to his nethers.

Acker's red face went white, and he scrambled away from me like I was on fire, his big body knocking against a stool at the island and dumping it over.

"Oh, so you believe me now? Good." I directed my attention to Linus. "Time for you to go. You don't have to cross over, but you can't stay here."

Linus appeared disappointed at his brother's reaction, his little shoulders drooping in defeat. "Can I stay in the yard maybe? Ambrose is my only family left. I don't want to turn bad."

A pang of hurt hit me, making me want to call Hildy or something. "The yard will be fine. And if you ever want to cross, let me know."

The little boy nodded like I'd given him a gift and winked out of sight.

Tobin shakily handed me a cup of coffee. It was black, but at this point I didn't really care. I gratefully took it from him and practically scalded my mouth sucking it down. When the cup was empty, I handed it back and turned to Bishop.

"Wards, then sleep?" I said on a yawn big enough to crack my jaw.

Bishop was still glaring at Acker like he wanted to rip the skin off his bones, but nodded, anyway. "I have the wards. You go to bed."

I wasn't going to argue.

Agent Yazzie guided me to the top floor, carrying my suitcase while Tobin struggled with the duffle full of weapons. I staggered up the steps, and when they indicated which room was mine and Bishop's, I fell into bed. My hair still smelled like smoke, and I needed a shower, but that bed called to me like a siren. As soon as the door closed, I managed to rifle through my suitcase for a set of sleep shorts, peel out of my jeans, and slap those suckers on before I was under the covers.

Sleep yanked me under before my head hit the pillow.

Though when I woke up, I wasn't in Knoxville anymore. When sleep finally released me, I was curled in a ball on top of a grave in Haunted Peak Memorial Cemetery.

Not good.

13

For about a minute, I honestly believed I was
dreaming. Why else would I be an hour away,
on top of a grave, in my pajamas? I'd been up
for ages and had no real rest before that—running on
empty for far too long. Why wouldn't I be dreaming?

But the longer I sat, the cold from the ground
seeping into my bones, the more I realized that I wasn't
asleep, and I wasn't dreaming, and I was really, really in
a cemetery in the middle of the night with no
recollection of how I got there.

And what was worse?

I was alone, barefoot, with no phone, in my fucking
pajama short-shorts on top of the very grave I'd been
drawn to hours before. My stomach pitched a little once
I figured out that part, too. Dew seeped into the fabric of

my clothes, the freezing wetness making my teeth chatter in my skull as the wind whipped through the trees. The fronds of the willow trees thrashed like strands of hair or like reaching fingers.

Stop it, Darby. Don't do this to yourself.

But my brain was now on a runaway train of intrusive thoughts and none of them were of the happy variety.

A stick snapped nearby, and I hopped to my feet, backing away from the gravestone before something worse happened. Sort of like the dark, ominous chuckle I could swear I heard floating through the trees.

Stumbling over my own bare feet, I scrambled out of the cemetery, nearly tripping on the chain that proclaimed the place was closed. Okay, so it was less of a scramble and more of a full-on sprint, my feet carrying me in whatever direction that was not deeper into that fucking graveyard.

Yes, even after everything I'd done—everything I'd been through—ghosts and spooky shit still freaked me out. It was true that I did see specters literally everywhere, every single day of my life. But that still didn't mean I wanted to meet one at night, and I sure as shit did not want to see one in the middle of the night in a *cemetery*.

Not just no, but fuck no.

When my legs decided to calm down, I was about two and a half miles into town. My feet were bloody and bruised, the sharp sting of the open wounds on the concrete finally filtering into my fool brain. Uncle Dave's house was three blocks north, Jimmy's cute cottage was ten blocks south, and my neighborhood—was about two more miles out.

Dave's house it was.

By the time I made it to Dave's house, I was a shivering, limping, freaked-the-fuck-out mess, made all the more so when I realized that Dave's street was filled to the damn brim with ghosts. Their glowing see-through bodies drifted closer and closer to me as I pounded on the wood.

My knuckles were raw by the time Uncle Dave ripped the door open, but I didn't give him a chance to say anything before I was shoving my way in his house.

"Shut the door," I hissed as I backed into his living room. The couch hit the back of my thighs and I lost my balance, plopping onto the oversized piece of furniture like a child.

As soon as my feet left the floor, the full weight of the trek here hit them—the throbbing, stinging, awful slamming into me all at once.

Dave swung the heavy wooden door shut, but didn't say a thing. Instead, he rubbed at his sleepy eyes as he let out a jaw-cracking yawn before clearing the chamber of the gun he evidently answered the door with.

"I could have sworn you were in Knoxville. I didn't dream that, right? And what in the hell happened to your feet? You didn't walk all the way here, did you?"

I inspected the state of my tootsies. I'd grown up running around barefoot just like every other kid, but I seriously doubted I could have walked the forty miles and only had this little damage. Don't get me wrong, my feet looked like hamburger, but not forty-miles worth. The blisters, oozing cuts, and rawness on the soles had to be from the sprint from the cemetery. So, if I didn't walk there—which I highly doubted I did—then how in the blue fuck did I end up on a grave when I was supposed to be sleeping in a nice cozy bed in Knoxville?

"I was," I croaked. "I was in Knoxville. I—" A shudder rocked through me, and I stole the throw blanket off the back of the couch. Unfortunately, I didn't have sense enough to wrap it around me and clutched the soft chenille to my chest like a pillow.

Dave approached, stowing his gun in a side table drawer and knelt at my feet.

"C-can you call Bishop? He must be worried sick." I wanted Bishop, sure, but I also wanted to hug someone —work out the problem with him, ask him for cocoa and his sweater, and beg for some bandages for my feet—but he wasn't here anymore, and it didn't feel right asking Dave for those things. Grief hit me in a one-two punch, and I swallowed so I wouldn't burst into tears on Uncle Dave's couch.

"Sure can, kiddo, but why don't you tell me what happened first?"

Shaking my head, I tried to clear the fog that had settled over my brain. "I don't know what happened. One second, I was asleep in Knoxville, and the next, I was in Haunted Peak Memorial Cemetery curled up on a grave. I don't—" My face crumpled, and it was all I could do to not start bawling right then and there. "Can you call Bishop, please?"

I shivered, the cold of the night still deep in my bones. Dave did that actual smart thing, and took the blanket from me, fanning it out so it settled on my shoulders. Then, he handed me a pillow, and I hugged it to my chest.

Okay, I might have snatched it, but this was serious.

"I'll make the call, all right?"

My nod was frantic as I whispered a pitiful, "Okay."

Uncle Dave left me then, likely to go find his phone, but the absence was hard regardless. Though, I wasn't alone for long. In a matter of about a minute, there was a wild-haired Bishop in his living room, complete with pajama pants, sleep shirt, and bare feet. One second the living room was empty, and the next, a waft of black smoke expelled Bishop like he'd been born from the darkness.

But his hair wasn't the only thing out of sorts in the room. His eyes were equally wild, the gold irises and harried set to them making him seem almost dangerous. Well, until he knelt at my feet.

Bishop seemed almost reluctant to touch me, so I threaded my fingers out of the blanket and reached for him. Immediately he took my hand, holding almost too tight as his hand trembled and his jaw clenched tight.

"What happened?"

Hot tears filled my eyes as I shook my head. "I don't know. The last thing I remember is falling asleep and then I woke up in the cemetery. I don't even know how I got there."

I had a handful of guesses as to what *could* have happened, but it seemed shitty to just spew them out. One theory rattling around in my head was that Acker had cursed me somehow, but honestly it wasn't the loudest one.

No, that was reserved for whatever Azrael had done to me when he'd kissed my forehead. He could just pop in wherever and whenever he wanted to. If he gave some of himself to me, wouldn't it make sense for me to just pop out of my bed to the first place I ever met him?

Okay, it was reaching, but it wasn't like I had a lot to go on.

Bishop nodded his head like a doctor about to give a pretty dire prognosis. "And why are you bleeding?"

Frowning, I peeled the blanket back to show him my feet and he hissed. "How did you know I was bleeding?"

Confused, he pointed to his chest. "Half blood mage, remember? I know a lot of things where that particular area is concerned." Gently, he took my left foot in his hand and inspected the damage. "This isn't fifty miles worth of damage—maybe a few miles. There's no way you walked here—especially in the short time you've been gone. That means you had to have transported yourself or someone did it for you. Is there anything significant to where you woke up?"

Swallowing hard, I nodded. "It's where I met Azrael for the first time."

A hint of relief hit Bishop's shoulders. "So it was likely you then. Maybe it's an ability manifesting itself for the first time. Considering you hate shade jumping so much, it could be a good thing."

Waking up in a graveyard didn't seem like a good thing to me, but being cursed was likely less so.

Dave returned to the living room carrying a wide basin of soapy water, a soft dark towel, and a black bag under his arm. Bishop took the pot from him and set it at my feet. Reluctantly, I immersed them, the sting setting my nerve endings on fire.

"Fates know what you picked up running here," Dave muttered. "Let's get you cleaned and bandaged, yeah?"

A plan. I liked plans. It made me feel some semblance of normal after all the crazy. I missed the days when I could come up with these plans, though. Missed when my whole world wasn't a giant dumpster fire, and I could handle shit by myself.

"Did you happen to look at the cases Yazzie and Tobin were going over?" Bishop asked, making a welcome subject change as I soaked my feet.

"No," I said, shaking my head. "I was barely conscious by the time I got to the Warden house. I think I had just enough gumption to knock Acker on his ass and that was about it."

A ghost of a smile crossed Bishop's face. "I looked them over while I was waiting for some of the wards to set. The most pressing had to do with a fire at the former ghoul nest home. It was mostly deserted, but there seemed to have been squatters that were caught in the blaze. Normally, we'd just start asking questions, but this one seems a bit more delicate."

I huffed. "Because I kicked them out of Knoxville?"

"No," Bishop replied, drawing out the word as his gaze shifted from me to Dave. "Because there was suspected wolf activity at the scene. There's word that a pack moved in the area once the ghouls split."

I sat back on the couch. "In two days? You're telling me that in two fucking days, a whole ass pack of wolves just decided to move to Knoxville on a whim?"

I'd expected Bishop to answer me, but it was Dave instead. "Not on a whim. The ghouls drove out the majority of the wolves about fifty years ago. With the ghouls gone, they likely took back their old residences." His gaze shifted to Bishop. "Though, this is all speculation since I don't have a pack, and you know that."

"Do you know the pack that moved back in?" Bishop asked. "Or have an in with them? Questioning anyone in the pack is going to be dicey. I know you are an Omega, but if we had an envoy, then..." Bishop trailed off when he realized Dave wasn't going to answer him.

Hell, I was fairly certain that if I hadn't claimed Bishop, Dave would be about four seconds away from chucking him out of the closest window. Dave crossed his arms over his chest, his jaw clenched in stone silence. As far as I knew, Omegas lived alone, refusing pack life altogether in favor of a solitary life. Which considering I hadn't known he was a wolf before a week ago, it made total sense.

"I'll talk to her. Not you. I've known that girl all her

life, and I know she wouldn't attack based on pure speculation. You? I don't know."

Bishop pursed his lips and returned to my feet, gently pulling them from the water and carefully drying them with the towel. "I get it. The ABI has a rep—and I'm not denying that it was earned—but I'm not them. I never wanted to be them."

He opened the black bag and spread ointment on the worst of the cuts.

"Five hundred years, La Roux. You had five centuries with them. All they've done, all they've taken. You've been a part of that."

Dave's words had Bishop's dark head nodding as he bandaged my wounds. "It was that or death. Sometimes I think death might have been a better option, but I'm free now. I get to make my own mistakes, my own rules."

"And when I think I can trust you, I'll talk to you. Until then, I'll be speaking to her."

Fair enough.

14

"It's time for you two to go," Dave muttered, staring at my feet instead of my face.

I couldn't tell if it was the set of his jaw or the turn of his shoulders, but I knew he was holding something back, not telling me something I needed to know. But I wouldn't get any answers with Bishop here, and Dave seemed about ready for us to skedaddle.

"Thanks for opening the door and getting me help and calling Bishop," I said as I gingerly rose to my feet. Bandaged, the pain wasn't too bad, but I'd need some pain meds if I planned on doing actual work. "Call me later when you feel up to it? We don't have to talk about anything you don't want to."

Reaching out a hand, I felt my whole body relax

when he actually took it. Dave had been in my life since I was a baby. There was no case that was going to come between us—I didn't care if he had the info or not.

"I know that, kiddo. Just… be careful, okay? Wolves are a messy bunch. They might look organized, but some of them would just as easily take you out rather than have you as a threat. There is a very good reason why I'm an Omega."

Dave wrapped me up in a hug and then let me go. He gave a rather half-hearted chin lift to Bishop and stepped back.

This was the part I'd been dreading. *Shade jumping.* Why didn't they just call it a "vomit comet" and be done with it. Bishop clutched me to his chest, took two steps toward a faint shadow, and then the world spun. Back in the day, there was this death trap of a carnival ride that was basically just a washing machine set to the spin cycle. No safety bars or seat belts, just a poor kid stuck to the side of a wall, using centrifugal force alone.

My dad had let me ride that ride exactly one time, and the pair of us vowed "Never again." That could have been because we both threw up hot dogs and funnel cake for what seemed like forever afterward, but that was just a theory.

Shade jumping felt like that ride times about a

million, and when we landed in a bedroom, Bishop
lurched for the closest trash can and handed it to me. I'd
had a penchant for tossing my cookies each time we did
this little song and dance, so at least the man was
prepared.

Fortunately—or unfortunately as the case was—I had
nothing in my stomach to toss, so all I got was dry
heaving as a bout of nausea for the trouble. I didn't care
how fast it was, I wouldn't be doing that again if
someone paid me.

I'd rather walk first.

When my heaving episode was over, Bishop thrust a
bottle of water in my hand, and I downed it in three
gulps, the icy goodness quelling my turbulent stomach.

"Tell me what really happened," he murmured,
peeling off his T-shirt and snagging another black one
from his bag.

Confused, I shook my head. "But I did."

He stuffed his head through the neck and shot me a
skeptical look. "Really? So, nothing happened at the
cemetery. Nothing spooked you or was significant in any
way. O-kay." Then he stripped off his pajama bottoms,
replacing them with dark-wash jeans.

A part of me wanted to snuggle into bed with him
and totally forget that I was supposed to be working.

The arcane world was mostly nocturnal, and I wasn't sure how much sleep I'd gotten, but I felt more rested than I had in days. True, that could be from the leftover adrenaline, but I doubted it.

I also debated whether or not I wanted to talk to him about what had me running from the graveyard in the first place. "Nope. Nothing remarkable at all."

Bishop sat next to me on the bed, his raised eyebrow practically weaponized it was so sharp. "Really?"

The skepticism in the air between us was palpable. "You're going to think I'm a wimp."

Bishop pressed his lips together to try and hide the smile on his lips, but failed miserably. "What happened?"

Shaking my head, I pulled the pillow from the top of the bed and hugged it to my middle. "I fell asleep here almost instantly. And then I woke up in the cemetery on the grave where I first met Azrael. Then the wind whipped through the trees and there was…"

Bishop must have had enough of my stalling because one second my ass was planted on the bed and I was seriously contemplating burying myself under the covers and never coming out again, and the next, he'd ripped the pillow out of my hands, and I was somehow on his lap.

"And there was what?" he murmured, his dark gaze boring a hole into me.

"Laughing. A deep, male chuckle floating through the trees. That's what had me running." I tore my gaze from his and settled on staring at my stupid bandaged feet. "I know it could have been anything. A bird, a ghost I didn't see, my own fear. But that's why I ran."

He gathered me closer, gently jostling me so I'd look at him. "I think we need to talk to Sarina. Maybe she can see what's going on."

Talking to our resident oracle would likely be the best course of action, but it felt weird that she was technically not Bishop's partner anymore—though I doubted she'd ever not be on our side, it was still a hurdle.

"If you—"

A knock rattled the bedroom door, cutting me off. "Warden Adler?"

Tobin's timid voice barely filtered through the wood, and I peeled myself from Bishop's hold to answer. Yanking the door open, I spied Tobin shaking like a leaf several paces away. "Yeah?"

"Umm... Sorry to bother you, but there has been another incident, and Director Davenport called, and he seems really mad—"

I held up a hand. "Take a deep breath for me, Aldrich. Can you do that?"

The wiry man kept wringing his hands as he took a shaky step forward. I gestured with my arms—the act of taking a deep breath—encouraging him to copy me. "In —one, two, three, four. And out—one, two, three four. Now, I need you to never call me Warden Adler in this house ever again."

I'd said it as mostly a joke, but it had the intended effect of making Tobin snort. "I can do that."

"Call me Darby or Adler. Let's save the Warden shit for people who don't live in this house, okay?" He gave me another shaky nod worthy of a bobblehead doll. "Now, I'll get dressed and then you can brief me on what happened, all right?"

Again with the nodding. "O-okay. I can do that. Do you want some coffee? Yazzie said you likely were on a dayshift schedule, though you did sleep for half a day, so—"

"Coffee would be good. Thank you," I said, cutting him off. Tobin had a habit of rattling on, and that was going to irk me to no end. I'd have to nip that in the bud soon in a way that didn't hurt his feelings since he was such a nice kid. Hurting his feelings would be like kicking a puppy.

"Oh, okay. Coffee," he muttered, nodding to himself as he turned to head down the stairs.

Closing the door, I moved back to Bishop. His eyes were all squinty like he was trying not to be pissed about something, but he was failing miserably.

"What?"

All expression wiped from his face in an instant, and he rose from the bed to snag a pair of fresh socks from his bag. "Nothing."

I snorted, reaching in my own bag for something to wear that wasn't pajama short-shorts and a T-shirt. "Sure. Now who's lying?"

Groaning, he said, "Fine. That kid has a crush on you. I mean, I get it. You're blonde and beautiful and a certified badass—any heterosexual man in their right mind would be. But he's just so... squirmy about it. Like he's fourteen and can't quit shooting off at the mouth."

Holding in my laugh was difficult, but I managed it as I selected a pair of black jeans, a black tank, and loose gray V-neck. But then my hands stilled as I went to lift my shirt.

"Do I have a badge or a service weapon? I mean you had a fake FBI badge, but I thought that was just to blend in. If I talk to authorities, am I going to have to bullshit them?"

Half the stuff I gleaned for arcane cases I'd only

gotten because I was a cop and had access. What the hell was I going to do if I didn't have a badge? Plus, it wasn't like I was too terribly good at lying in the first place. I got out of most situations by not talking at all.

Bishop snorted as he threaded his belt through the loops of his jeans. "Tobin dropped off your badge while you were sleeping. You'll be a fake Fibbie like I was. Local cops usually don't ask questions, anyway. Unless they're stingy ghost-seeing homicide detectives, that is."

Relief and a bit of warmth filled me. Bishop had posed as an FBI agent when we'd first met, trying to steal one of my cases. Granted, said case involved an evil death-dealing sorceress and a dead body with my business card in her hand, but that was not the point.

I stuck my tongue out at him and got busy with the dressing. By the time I was done, he'd brushed his teeth and stuffed his feet into a pair of shoes. He dropped a kiss to my lips and left me to the rest of my preparations —which wasn't much. In the en suite bathroom, I, too, brushed my teeth, wrangled my hair up in a haphazard ponytail, and stared at myself in the mirror for about a solid minute.

Since Azrael's healing gift, I hadn't spent too much time cataloging the differences in my appearance, and the change was more than a little noticeable. My hair was white. Not blonde, not gray. White. Even the little baby hairs at my temples and nape were paler than the driven snow. By comparison, my skin seemed practically tan.

Okay, in no way would I ever be considered tan, but still.

The dark purple bags under my eyes that I'd just assumed were permanent were long gone, and the scar over my right eyebrow—that I'd gotten from J in the fifth grade—was conspicuously absent. My eyes seemed bluer, my skin smoother.

It was fucking unsettling, and I didn't like it.

Though, I didn't need the concealer in my makeup bag, just a spot of mascara and lip balm. It made me feel less human, less like I was Killian's, and the thought twisted my stomach in knots. Without another look at the mirror, I left the bathroom and gingerly got my feet into a pair of thick socks and sturdy leather boots, adding a matching leather belt and spine holster, and snagging my rosaries for good measure.

I'd always felt odd about the trio of blessed rosaries Dave had given me on my thirteenth birthday. Every so often, I got the blessings renewed by a local priest. I couldn't say whether or not the necklaces helped keep away bad spirits or acted as a good luck charm, but the fact that I'd survived thus far with them on my person seemed to lend to that notion. It wasn't like I believed in what they represented, either. After what I'd been through, believing in any one religion seemed short-sighted. But what did I know?

Not a damn thing.

I filled my spine holster with my favorite nine-millimeter and snagged a jacket.

My first real day as Warden.

Man, I hope I don't fuck it up.

15

I *am so going to fuck this up.*

Staring at the still-raging inferno that used to be the Dubois vampire nest's former home, I was pretty sure I was in over my head. Both great spires of the cathedral had nearly collapsed as the smoke poured into the night sky.

Word from the firefighters on scene was that the fire was far too hot, and no one could enter for fear that their suits wouldn't protect them. Considering we were on the arcane side of town—not that the humans knew that—the likelihood that the blaze was magical in nature was almost a certainty. The human authorities on scene suspected there had been people caught in the inferno, but I didn't need to guess.

The small contingent of specters told the tale far better than they could.

Ingrid is going to be so pissed.

My small vampire friend was going to shit Frisbees when she got word that her nests' home had been defiled. Granted, the nest had taken temporary residence elsewhere after a nasty battle some weeks back, so at least it wasn't my friends that were crispy critters.

Has it been weeks?

I tried to fit all that had happened into the small bit of time and came up empty. Fighting shoulder to shoulder with Ingrid had to have been years ago, not weeks, but what did I know?

Questioning the ghosts themselves would be dicey, though. With all the law enforcement officers and firemen and slew of onlookers around, I was going to have to get creative with how I did it, too. Day one and already it was a mess.

Fabulous.

"Miss? I'm going to need you to stand back. We're clearing this area of civilians," a beat cop with all the audacity of a mediocre white man instructed, totally ignoring the two men standing on either side of me. I knew I was a tall lady, but Bishop and Yazzie were hard to miss, and he went around all six feet and some change of Bishop to come right to me.

Unclipping the totally fake but very real-looking FBI badge from my belt, I held it up, not even bothering to look him in the eye. "Not a civilian." Reclipping the badge, I gave him my best death glare. "Go away."

I knew of cops like this—the ones who should have either never taken the job in the first place or just refused to learn with the times. There had been plenty of them when I started the force, but luckily Cap had weeded most of them out. Here, not so much.

"You ca—" the cop sputtered, and I held up a hand.

Leaning forward, I checked to see if there were other LEOs at about the same distance from the fire as we were. Since we were actually farther back, I shifted my gaze to Bishop. "It's the hair, isn't it?"

Bishop's lips tugged into a sly smile like he was waiting for me to lay into the guy. "Probably."

"It could also be your youthful appearance," Yazzie chimed in, leaning over to stage whisper. "Or the general air of zero fucks. It's a toss-up, really."

It was times like this that I missed J. There was nothing wrong with Bishop or Yazzie, but J would have raised a single eyebrow and sent this dude running for his mommy. If he didn't leave me alone, I would have to tattle to his supervisor, and then it was going to turn into a jurisdiction pissing match. I just didn't want to have to deal with that at one thirty in the fucking morning, thank you very much.

Sighing, I pinched the bridge of my nose. "Look, sweetie," I said in my most saccharine Southern accent —the one I used on assholes and people I didn't like. "I don't care what you think I can and can't do. I'm staying here, and unless it's a safety issue, I'm going to need you to fuck on off, mm-kay? Can you do that for me? Thank you."

Talking to the handful of specters was going to be bad enough, I didn't need sexist douche canoes added to it.

The officer's face got red as his mouth formed a solid line. With a growl befitting an enraged teenage girl, he stormed off to the next group of people, barking at them to get behind the haphazard barricade made from police tape and collapsible metal barriers.

One down, one to go.

Before I was out of the grave talker closet, I would pretend to be talking on the phone while I questioned a specter. The act allowed me to speak freely while making sure I didn't get a grippy sock vacation. Being involuntarily committed to a mental facility seemed like a bad plan for someone who could see ghosts. Well, hospitals in general were not my favorite places—they were a teensy step up from cemeteries in the ghost department.

Specters tended to stick around the places where they'd died or where their bodies rested, so hospitals, mental facilities, prisons, and yes, graveyards were all on my no-no list.

"Okay," I said, sighing, "how does this incident compare to the Monroe nest fire?"

Yazzie tilted his head to the side and sniffed the air. "The fire and smoke mask a lot of scents, so without witnesses we won't know for sure if it is the same people. In fact, had we not gotten a wolf track at the ghoul scene, we wouldn't have known it was them. As far as similarities, I believe the same accelerant was used, though it seems to have been mixed with what I assume is witch magic. The Knoxville police say there were no witnesses, so that's a bust."

No witnesses. I huffed out a mirthless chuckle. "There *are* witnesses—just not any living ones."

I stared at the gaggle of specters that huddled together at the front of the building. Since the area where they were congregating was actively on fire, it wasn't like I could just stroll on over and get the scoop. And then there was the other thing...

"What do you need?" Bishop muttered, seeming to sense my hesitation.

It wasn't that I didn't want to talk to the specters.

I did.

In theory.

More, it was that the thought of calling any spirit to me made me want to hurl. Before the whole "fill Darby with thousands of souls" thing, I could call or push souls away—no problem. Now? I wasn't sure if I even wanted to try it.

Azrael was gone. If I fucked it up, took in too many souls, or generally screwed something up, there wasn't much of a backup system in place. Yes, Sloane was around somewhere, but using her as a fuck-up crutch after what she'd already gone through could be classified as a dick move on my part.

I could figure this out. I could. *Couldn't I?*

"A safe, non-populated area to call the specters to me and the gumption to not royally fuck it up." Yes, I said that out loud with Yazzie just standing right there listening. At least I was being up front about how much of a shitshow I'd be running, so there was that.

"There's a park right across the street. Will that work?" Yazzie offered, pointing to a spot in the distance.

A dark, deserted public park at night? Sounded like a super-awesome place to talk to a handful of specters.

I fought off a shudder and marched in the direction he'd pointed, mentally leaving breadcrumbs for the gaggle of ghosts to follow me. I had half a mind to call Hildy to me so he could talk me through this shit, but again, there was that little tidbit about not relying on people.

As the distance from the fire grew, a chill swept through my body, causing all my baby hairs to rise on end.

Get it together, Darby.

Reluctantly, I checked over my shoulder, hoping the spirits decided to get wise and follow. Fortunately—or unfortunately considering actually talking to them was going to suck—their glowing, see-through forms shone like beacons as they drifted closer and closer to me. I made my feet keep a sedate pace, refusing to let them fly down the sidewalk. Not only did I suspect that would feel absolutely horrific on my cut-up feet, but it would also likely make me look like a complete nutter.

I stopped at the closest bench and sat, doing my best not to flinch when they got too close. The first spirit was a familiar-looking brunette, her features reminding me of a wi—

"You," the witch-bitch growled, drifting nearer to the bench but not getting too close. "I can't believe you actually killed us. We were just following orders."

My back hit the seat in affront—or it could have been her ghostly friends swarming me like bees. I pushed back with my mind, the memory of the lake lashing a bitter sort of pain through me. When I'd threatened to take out any Knoxville coven witch on sight, I was dead serious, but I'd at least given them a head start. If she got killed in a place she most definitely was not supposed to be, that wasn't my fucking problem.

And if I'd actually killed her, I would be claiming it. Gladly.

"Following orders wasn't a good enough reason not to prosecute the Nazis, and it's not a viable defense for your actions, either. And you weren't following orders. You wanted that power just as much as everyone at that lake did, and that's why you got a death threat. But much to my dismay, I didn't kill you, so why don't you tell me what you saw so I can find the person who did?"

And maybe send them a fruit basket for taking out the trash.

Her name filtered into my brain. Simone something. Dumond, Drummond, Duncan… I knew her last name started with a "D."

"You sent those dogs after us," she hissed, putting her ghostly hands on her hips. I always found it strange that ghosts presented themselves as they wanted to be seen. This lady likely died as a crispy critter, but her spirit was a picture of health, no bites or burns or anything to suggest her death was gruesome or painful. That didn't mean it hadn't been—it just didn't show.

And dogs? By George, I think we have a link to the ghoul fire.

"I didn't send any dogs after you," I replied, shooting a look at Bishop. "And again, what happened? You accusing me isn't telling me anything and I've got other places to be. Maybe one of your friends would like to tell me who killed her?"

Out of the group of female witches, there were one or two that seemed inclined to speak to me, the shy one still wearing glasses in the afterlife being the one I'd pick. Clearing my head, I tried to call her forth in my mind, pulling that tiny tether that seemed to connect me to all deceased souls.

She came freely, but her name was a mystery. She didn't look familiar, either. Her hair had been blonde or maybe light brown in life—a sharp contrast to her darker skin. It surrounded her head in a halo of carefully crafted ringlets. Her eyes were pale behind the glasses—maybe light hazel or green in life, and her style was decidedly '90s grunge but with a modern flair. Personally, I'd shank someone for the ability to pair a flowy dress and thick combat boots, but dresses and I didn't get along.

Mentally, I tried to shove Simone back, but that bitch was tenacious.

"You can't get rid of me. I know you had a hand in this." Simone had the definite possibility of turning into a poltergeist—the rage poured from her in waves that had her form flickering as her head rolled on her neck. Even the ghosts around her started to give her space as they waited for her to blow.

But I was just done. Done with talking to a ghost that had wronged me in life. Done with spending even a second's energy on calming her down. Hell, if it hadn't been for Bishop and Yazzie—the latter of which seemed freaked all the way out—I wouldn't have bothered.

"But I didn't. Until yesterday I'd been mourning my father. Remember the man ya'll killed? I haven't so much as attempted to sniff you and yours out. I didn't kill you. I didn't ask anyone to kill you. I didn't pay anyone to kill you. And as much as I wanted you dead, I wanted to be the one to do it more. So start talking or get the fuck out of the way before I send you to Hell where you belong."

That did the trick. Simone backed up, her rage dialing down to zero as the threat of Hell became a real possibility.

Directing my attention to the calm witch, I asked, "What's your name, darling?"

She shot me a smile. "Lucy. And I'm sorry to hear about your dad. I didn't know."

A realization hit me. "You weren't a member of the coven, were you?"

Lucy shook her head. "Not before a few days ago.

The word around the witch community is that you banned all witches in Knoxville, and a bunch of them are gathering new members to strike at you."

It was tough not to roll my eyes, but I managed it. "Actually, I only banned the *one* coven, but that's only because they tried to crack open the Underworld and steal its power. They also killed my dad, kidnapped my best friend, and tried to use me as a supernatural ghost battery, so I kind of felt the banning was warranted."

Lucy's eyes got so big in her head that I thought they might pop out. "They did what? No one is saying that. No one knows."

"I'm gathering that. But why don't you tell me what happened to you?" I'd fix my own issues someday, but this girl's life had been stolen, and I wanted to find the person who did it.

Lucy shook her head—less like she was disagreeing and more like she was trying to reorder her thoughts. "We were doing an induction. I wasn't sure I wanted to be a member. Simone just seemed like she wanted numbers and not power, but no other covens wanted me. I wasn't very good at spells, but I could grow plants like nobody's business. I heard growling and then…"

She frowned like she was trying to remember the rest. "Something hit me, big and dark and so fast. I couldn't move—my body wouldn't…" Her breath shuddered in her chest, spectral tears falling down her cheeks. "Then the flames came."

"You were alive when you burned," I offered before swallowing hard. This girl had been innocent. She'd been a good kid caught up with bad people and paid with her life. "I'm so sorry, Lucy. You didn't deserve that." I shifted my attention to the other witches. "You were killed in the same manner?"

A blonde approached. "I didn't burn, but I saw a dog or a wolf or something. It went for my throat. I think it broke my neck."

Another of the group nodded, a haunted expression on her pale face. "It was a wolf—three of them. They attacked fast. I don't think they knew we were going to be there because the fire started first. I tried to get out when I got caught."

Trying and failing to not grind my teeth, I nodded. "Thank you. I appreciate ya'll talking to me." I turned to Yazzie. "The wolf pack you suspect have a penchant for killing innocent women by way of ripping out their throats?"

Sure, Simone wasn't innocent, but these other girls? They didn't deserve this.

Yazzie took a step back. "That is how a wolf typically kills, yes, but a pack member's honor wouldn't allow them to—"

"Murder seven women? Witness statements say different. I think we need to talk to some wolves, what do you think?"

Yazzie took another step back, shooting me a look of utter horror. "I think that's a horrible idea."

Was it a terrible idea? Probably.

Was I going, anyway?

You're damn right I was.

16

I t took some convincing, but Yazzie coughed up his top three locations where he thought the wolves might be holing up. It was less convincing and more me silently staring at him until he caved, but whatever.

"You really are planning on going into a wolf den, and what? Asking the bad guys to just politely come with you? Are you out of your mind?" Yazzie asked, his carefully constructed outer calm destroyed.

Bishop snorted and marked the third location on a map—an actual paper map of the city of Knoxville and the surrounding area that he'd pulled from his go bag in my Jeep and spread across the hood. "She calls the vampire queen of Knoxville Mags, for fuck's sake. Of course she is."

I rolled my eyes and looked at the three dots. Two were farther inside the city limits without access to open land for running. The third went up against the national forest preserve. If I was a betting woman, that's where I'd set up camp. Though, my knowledge of wolf behavior was limited at best.

Pointing to the spot, I asked, "This is probably it, right? Open land for running, room to expand, less natural predators, and more food. Granted, it's harder to defend, but if they have the numbers, that isn't really an issue."

Yazzie narrowed his eyes at me. "I thought you said you didn't know anything about wolves."

"That doesn't mean I'm an idiot or that pop culture hasn't taught me a little. Wolves are the wilder of the weres, right?"

He crossed his arms and tilted his head to the side, assessing me. "Yeah."

"Then they act more like actual wolves than say coyotes or werecats do with their species, right?" I got a chin lift in the affirmative. "If I was a wolf, I'd want open space to run and food. City dwelling doesn't offer it, so..." I pointed to the spot on the map. "Duh."

"And you need me because, why again? Because I have no desire to go get torn apart by a bunch of wolves. No job is worth that, thank you."

Yazzie brought up a good point, but I had an answer. "Do packs hunt in small contingents of two or three, or do they go about twenty-deep for security?" I had a feeling they didn't, which leant toward the idea that it wasn't the pack as a whole, but a small faction.

"You seem to already know the answer to that."

I nodded. "And if you were the head of your pack—"

"An alpha."

"—wouldn't you want to know that some outliers were about to start a war? If I was in charge, I for damn sure would want that knowledge. I'll be polite and respectful."

The tall agent gave me the side-eye. "This coming from a woman that broke an agent's nose less than a day ago."

Shrugging, I smiled. "That was Acker's own fault, and you know it. He thought I was a pushover. I taught him otherwise. If he's smart, he won't make the same mistake twice."

Yazzie sighed. "Fine. I'll give you a rundown of wolf customs and courtesies, but that's it. I'm not going in there."

"That's the spirit," I said, slapping him on the arm.

. . .

The perimeter of the wolves' property seemed heavily fortified for a group of people who'd moved in two days ago. Wrought-iron fencing was topped with barbed spikes, and stone pillars every twenty or so feet. Cameras had been installed recently, too, and painted to blend in with the faux ivy draped over the stone. There was zero chance of me scaling that fence and an even slimmer one of me doing it undetected.

Moved in two days ago, my ass.

My headlights caught the eyes of the four wolves pacing around the gate—two inside and two out. There had to have been more I couldn't see, but this small group was plenty.

"I feel like a dog treat joke would be remiss here," I muttered, and Bishop snorted.

"Agreed, but you know they can hear you, right?" he said, covering his mouth with his hand.

The wolf closest to my Jeep bared its teeth and snarled.

Duly noted.

Shaking my head, I opened the car door and stepped out, moving slowly to the hood and parking my ass on the bumper. The wolf eyed me with an expression I could only interpret as irritated.

"I was kidding. If you were a real puppy, I'd be feeding you meat and trying to scale that fence," I admitted, earning myself a snap of teeth and a hair-raising growl for the trouble. "Since you're not, I'm just going to sit here and politely ask to speak to your alpha."

All four wolves growled then as if I'd said something horrible and I fought off the urge to roll my eyes. "Oh, give it a rest before I find a rolled-up newspaper. I would like to speak to your alpha, but I will gladly speak to an emissary if he is unavailable. And I'm going to sit here until someone speaks to me, so you can bitch and moan all you want to, but I'm not moving."

The dog closest to me snapped his sharp teeth about a foot from my leg, but Yazzie had taught me well on the thirty-minute drive out to the sticks. I didn't so much as flinch, and instead, looked him right in the eye and raised a single eyebrow.

"You bite me and I'm snapping your fool neck, pup. Don't play with me."

The two wolves inside the gate whined a little, and one of them took off for the house that had to be hidden behind a boatload of darkness and a literal forest of trees. It took an age, but eventually the shape of a man filtered through the dim light. He was dressed casually much like I was, a thin T-shirt and jeans, leather jacket and beanie. His dark skin gleamed against the headlights, but it was his eyes that really caught my attention. They were dark brown, almost black, but the shine of the headlights bounced back, making them damn near reflective like a cat's.

He kept walking even as he approached the gate, and the wrought iron opened seemingly of its own accord. I knew it wasn't magic, but it did have all the little hairs on my arms standing on end.

"Warden Adler," the man effused, his tone perfectly polite, but there was an edge there, too. He didn't want me here, that much was certain. "How may I be of assistance?"

I gave him my very best "butter wouldn't melt in my mouth" smile. "I appreciate you taking the time to speak with me. I would like to speak with the alpha if possible. There have been a few incidents with I believe three of this pack's wolves, and I would very much like to resolve it before the ABI gets involved."

The man's eyes glowed blue for a second as he sniffed the air. "It seems the ABI is already involved," he said, nodding to my Jeep. "I see two in your vehicle."

"One," I corrected, "but they both work for me for the time being."

He seemed to mull that over. "Fair enough. *You* may come with me, but the mage and the bear stay."

Bear?

I whipped my head around to stare through the

windshield. Yazzie was a *bear*? I'd have to tease him about that later. Then his decree filtered through my brain, and I winced. That wince turned into an almost groan when Bishop exited the Jeep, his face like a coming storm.

"I don't think so," Bishop growled, his tone so much like one of those wolves it gave me chills. "There is no reality where Warden Adler is going anywhere without backup."

The wolves flanking the man growled and snapped as he raised his nose in the air and took a giant sniff. "I don't care if she's your girlfriend, you aren't permitted."

The laugh that came out of Bishop La Roux was just a single step shy of completely unhinged. "Do you have any idea how many bodies are buried in these hills, sir? Thousands, their bones just begging me to raise them. Do you know what I can accomplish with just a handful? She does not go in alone. Not ever."

Out of all the people to have as backup, Bishop La Roux was at the top of the list, and the fact that he was ready to put it all on the line, made me want to jump his bones. But later. When the threat of death wasn't so real.

The man lifted one side of his mouth in a sly smile, raising his eyebrows as he nodded to the car. "Fair enough. You may enter with your woman, but again, the bear stays here."

I snorted. "Not a problem."

When we were never seen again, *someone* needed to call the authorities, and that someone was Jensen Yazzie.

"Follow me."

The instruction wasn't exactly necessary. Following him was the only option, as we started off into the darkness.

The faint traces of the mammoth home started to filter through the night about five minutes into our trek down the winding two-rut lane. Torches dotted the manicured lawn as it yawned wide, illuminating a three-story home with giant columns and deep verandas. There were shadowy traces of outbuildings, but the main attraction was an oversized double-door entrance with a wolf head carved into the wood.

We followed at a more clipped pace once we entered the home, the man—who'd never introduced himself—moved through the hallway and into what I assumed was a parlor or den of some sort. At the back of the room was an empty wooden chair. Covered in fur pelts with two wolves lounging on either side, the chair could only be classified as a throne.

And the man sat on it.

Of course he did.

Yazzie had gone on and on about wolf etiquette—namely how to act when an alpha was present. Don't make eye contact, don't sass him, and for all that was holy, don't threaten. Bishop and I had done all three, which made the fact that we were supposed to bow right about then seem a bit moot.

Bishop—as expected—did the whole kneel and bow thing. I did not. Instead, I crossed my arms and raised a single eyebrow and waited for him to fucking well introduce himself. I supposed he didn't really need to. Yazzie had already told us his name.

Cassius Leblanc and his pack had been summarily kicked out of Tennessee about fifty years ago back when the vampires, witches, and ghouls actually worked together. Uncle Dave had said it was the ghouls alone, but Yazzie gave us the ABI version of the story.

Evidently, Mr. Leblanc had a little trouble keeping his wolves in line, and far too many of them were accused of mauling humans and arcaners alike. Killing a whole pack for the actions of a few was something the ABI was not interested in, so the factions of Knoxville had driven them out. Or at least that was how the story went in the ABI files. I'd found time and time again that the truth was likely somewhat different, so I was willing to give this alpha the benefit of the doubt.

For now.

Cassius gave me a blindingly white grin—one that had the likely intended effect of showing me all his teeth —before a chuckle slipped from his lips. In the light, he seemed older than I'd originally thought, though I knew he had to be centuries if not more than I'd peg a human with his features. The thing that distinguished him as anything older than what he looked was the trace of white in his black beard.

"My son bet me a thousand dollars that you would not bow to me."

I snorted. "It sounds like your son might actually know me."

Then puzzle piece after puzzle piece fell into place right before the set of double doors to the south of the room opened. Uncle Dave and Sarina walked through them, followed by six very large men and four equally formidable women.

"I believe that he does," Cassius replied, and I couldn't decide if I was supremely lucky to have backup already inside with me or utterly and completely fucked.

Only time would tell.

17

There were only so many options for how to navigate a delicate situation, such as the one I had found myself in. I could act like seeing my father's best friend—and evident werewolf royalty— just stroll into his father's home was no big deal and this was all going according to plan. I could freak. Or I could choose none of the above and do nothing.

I was a fan of the "nothing" option. It hid any fear I had, made me look like a badass, and it didn't give anything away.

Unfortunately, Bishop did not get that memo.

He stood, narrowing his eyes at Dave like he was ready to attack him in the middle of a wolf den and beat his ass. "All speculation, huh? Good to know the trust you have in Darby goes both ways. Wouldn't want to get blindsided, now, would we?" His gaze drifted to Sarina. "I expected better out of you."

Sarina's amber eyes narrowed to slits. "And I expected to not have to come and save your ass after you left the ABI, but here the fuck I am."

I pinched my brow as Bishop and Sarina started bickering like an old married couple.

Children. I am dealing with fucking children.

I mean, it was damn near three-ish in the morning, and these three idiots were arguing in front of a man that no one in their right mind wanted to reveal a weakness to, and I was just done.

D-O-N-E, done.

I fit two fingers in my mouth like my dad taught me, and blew a whistle so loud, everyone including the alpha shuddered.

"Are you quite finished?" I hissed before stomping off to snatch a spindly-looking hardback chair from a rather bare table at the side of the room. Dragging it back to where I'd been standing, I then slammed the wood onto the stone and plopped onto it.

In all honesty, I just wanted to talk to the alpha and get this over with so I could get some coffee or food or sleep—maybe all three. Innocent women had died for crying out loud—had that escaped everyone's attention?

"Now where were we? Oh, that's right. Uncle Dave

is your son, Agent Kenzari is here because she needs to be, and you and I were about to speak about the murders and arson, is that correct?"

"Murders and arson? You said incidents. I would not classify murders and arson as mere incidents, Warden Adler, would you?" Cassius asked, shifting in his seat.

I mirrored him, shifting to the left and crossing my legs, resting my head on a single index finger. "At the time I had no idea you were the alpha. And incident can mean a great many things, but none of them are exactly happy."

"Fair enough. Carry on."

I shot a look at Dave to gauge his reaction, but he gave me nothing. "Over the last forty-eight hours, there have been two major fires at arcane nests. The former Monroe nest home and the Dubois nest. At the Monroe nest there were three human deaths from what we believe to be transients being trapped in the blaze. Wolf prints were discovered at the scene. The Dubois fire took the lives of several witches who were hiding in the abandoned building. They were attacked by three wolves before their necks were broken or torn out completely. One of them didn't die right away, and she burned alive, unable to move or call out for help."

Straightening, I gave the alpha my coldest stare. "Seven women and three men are dead. Two major fires.

Human eyes on the cases. We have a problem, sir. Or rather, you have a problem."

Because wolves could be placed at both scenes, because it was only a matter of time before human cops came knocking on their door, because if I didn't squash this, Davenport was going to do something stupid.

"I was under the impression the Dubois fire was still raging. How do you know this—the women, how they died?" Cassius leaned forward in his seat, a faint blue glow to his irises.

"Do you know what I am?"

Cassius shook his head. "You don't smell of anything I've ever seen before."

The smile on my face was bitter. "That's because there's no one like me. My mother was a grave talker, and my father was the Angel of Death. You could say that speaking to the dead is kind of my area of expertise. So, I don't need to wait for the coroner or an exam—not when I can just talk to the women who were murdered."

Cassius' face paled slightly. "And they tell you the truth, these ghosts?"

"Yes. In the end, there is no hiding from me." Where that had come from, I wasn't sure, but it sounded about right. "Now, I personally believe that you couldn't have known about the fires or what a small group of your wolves were up to. Packs are large, and policing everyone is impossible. But you could help me find the wolves responsible. We could make sure they don't do this again—don't hurt innocent people again."

The alpha nodded. "And how do you expect me to find these wolves?"

I wanted to say that I didn't give a shit how he found them, but that wasn't exactly true. I probably cared about it—or at least I would if innocent people kept getting killed. "Well," I said, mirroring his posture and sitting forward in my seat, "you can use your knowledge of your pack to deduce the culprits, or I can call Magdalena and Ingrid Dubois and they can start looking for who burned their cathedral to the ground. Now, one of those options is going to start a war, and I think you know which one of them it is."

I wasn't stupid enough to cross Ingrid let alone Mags, and I hoped he wasn't, either.

A woman behind me spat something in French, practically growling at her alpha. My French was a little rusty, but it sounded a whole hell of a lot like "Fuck the vampire scum" or something sort of like it.

"One down and two to go?" I muttered, and Cassius tipped his chin up while clucking his tongue.

The two wolves on either side of him stood before a pale mist enveloped their bodies. When the mist cleared, two giant men stood in their stead, their eyes glowing blue. Then the men moved, fast as lightning they had the woman on her knees in between the alpha's chair and mine. She was muscular and probably as tall as I was, her long legs encased in leather pants that seemed to only be held together by the ties that ran along her thighs. Her auburn hair was pulled into a mohawk-style braid at the center of her head, and her makeup was done up in Viking-style war paint.

She struggled against their holds, but she was no match for the big men.

"You smell of smoke, Gemma," Cassius cooed. "Were you somewhere you should not have been?"

How will I find them? Sure. I fought off the urge to roll my eyes.

Gemma had the audacity to spit at her alpha's feet. "You have us come back here only once the ghouls were gone. Then you say we have to abide by the rules. We have to play nice. We cannot take revenge for what was stolen from us. That home, that cathedral, those used to be ours. If we could not take them back, I made sure those who betrayed us could not have them, either."

I knew the ABI report had left a lot of shit out. It also had me wondering what other properties used to belong to the wolves. I was willing to bet the Knoxville coven house might have been on that list.

"You endanger us, child. You put every single one of

us at risk by perpetuating this lie. We left because it was that or face the council for what your father and brothers had done. We lost everything because your family went rabid. Your brothers paid for their mistakes with their lives, but the whole pack suffered. We went from the most prominent wolf pack in the Americas to what we are now, and you risk it all—risk us all—for some perceived slight that isn't even true."

"They were ours—"

"Those properties were repayment. Recompense for the lives taken. And you burned them to the ground—killing humans and witches alike along the way." Cassius stared at the woman like she was the foulest thing in the entire world. "And you brought your younger brothers with you."

That had me sitting up.

"They are children, Gemma. How could you?" A woman called from the middle of the group, shock and hurt on her face. She had the same auburn hair, the same green eyes, and the same tall build as Gemma, but I couldn't tell if she was her sister or mother. "Bran and Reynard are only twelve."

Cassius clucked his tongue again, and three people left the room.

"They should know, Mother. They should know what our blood has died for."

The woman marched up to her daughter and slapped her right across the face. "Your brothers died for a lie. A stupid lie propagated by men too small to realize there are plenty of seats at the table for everyone. Wolves are no better than other weres, and we are no better than other arcaners. Your father and brothers killed people for sport, as a game. They were cruel and vile, and I never hid the truth from you. I thought... I thought I'd gotten through to you."

Disgust pulled her lips downward before she took a knee at the alpha's feet. "Do what you must, my King."

The doors opened again, and the three men were accompanied by two small redheaded boys. They were skinny and scared and confused.

"Mom? Gemma?" the boy on the right whimpered, while the one on the left seemed to understand.

Cassius looked at the two boys, assessing them as a spider would a fly. Then he shifted to face me. "I'll make you a deal, Warden. I will let the ABI arrest these boys if and only if you can take down Gemma." He paused, and I waited because I knew it wasn't over. "If you can't take her down, I will kill them all and wipe their seed from my pack."

"Da—"

"No, wa—"

Dave and Bishop advanced forward, but I held up a

hand, still staring at the alpha. Yazzie warned me about this. Hell, it was half the reason he didn't want me to come at all. Wolves were considered the fiercest, most ruthless of the weres. The most animalistic. If someone —pack member or no—threatened the safety and security of the group as a whole, they were culled without a second thought.

But I didn't want those children's deaths on my hands—no matter what they had done. Did I think they deserved to be punished? Absolutely. But I had a feeling Gemma had more than a little to do with the actual murdering than these two.

My gaze shifted to the boys. "Did you take their throats, or did you start the fire?"

Neither was better, but if these boys could be spared, then I was going to do it.

The one on the left swallowed hard, his eyes flicking back and forth from me to his alpha and then to Gemma. "Bran was outside keeping an eye out. Gemma said she wanted to make sure no one got hurt because in the ghoul house there had been bums inside and we hadn't known. She went in first—" Tears filled his eyes as he shook his head. "I heard the screams. Bran and I went in, and Gemma was going for a girl. She took her throat. I told Bran that they were bad people, but I knew what she'd done. But he didn't know. He didn't know."

How could they, after the deaths they knew about... they still went ahead and... I wanted to puke. So many lives destroyed. Was this what being Warden was going to be?

"Agreed. I'll take her down, and the ABI arrests Bran and Reynard. They will get their tribunal." Whether or not it would be fair was another matter entirely. I also didn't add that Gemma was on the chopping block no matter what happened. That many lives lost, there was no way the ABI would let her live.

I think we both knew that.

"Claws and weapons?" I asked, getting the lay of the rules.

"Claws and blades. No guns," the alpha countered.

I shrugged. "Magic and spells?"

"Allowed. Try not to blow up my home, though."

Snorting, I muttered, "No promises."

"Fair enough."

18

Standing from my chair, unhurried, I sauntered over to Bishop, pulling off my jacket. I passed over the gun at my spine and the one at my ankle. Then I yanked out one of the trio of blades I kept at my other ankle, and spun it around my thumb to get a better grip.

"Are you fucking crazy?" Bishop hissed, tucking my gun and jacket under his arm. "She's going to tear you apart." But there was a gleam in his eyes—one that said he was only saying this so my opponent would hear him.

Sneaky bastard.

"Of course I'm crazy," I replied, giving a sidelong glance to Sarina. She winked and faced forward, and I returned my gaze to Bishop. "I love you, don't I?"

Dave nearly shoved Bishop out of the way. "What do

you think you're doing, Darby? Wolves are not to be messed with. Did this one just murder seven women? What would your father think about this?"

For a moment, I'd almost forgotten Dad was gone. Almost blocked out the fact that I wasn't going to see him again.

"My dad can't think anything about this because he's dead, David. Any other sore subjects you want to bring up right before I go into a fight, or are you done?"

Dave grabbed my arm nearly hard enough to bruise. "Killian wanted me to protect you. He woul—"

Darkness clouded my vision for a second, and when I blinked again, Dave was on his ass, cradling the hand that had been on my arm. "Dad wanted me to be safe, but in the end, he knew I could take care of myself. He was proud of me."

Or at least that's what I hoped the note he'd given Sloane said. I still hadn't read it, and I didn't know if I ever could.

Turning my back on the lot of them, I returned to the center of the room. Gemma was still bookended by the two guards, a sort of false sneer on her lips. I couldn't say I really blamed her for that expression. I could totally blame her for the fires, murders, and pain she'd caused, but the sneer? Not so much. We both knew she wouldn't be making it out of this room. She wouldn't be escaping. And it didn't matter one way or the other, unless she actually gave a shit about her family.

That part was debatable.

I suspected Cassius was trying to gauge her honor. An honorable person would fold, allowing herself to be taken rather than let her brothers die beside her, but I had a tiny inkling in my gut that Gemma was not honorable, nor did she give a ripe shit about her brothers.

Gemma cared about herself and only herself.

As soon as the guards dropped their hands, my suspicions were proved right. The phase hit her in an instant, the auburn-haired beauty disappearing almost immediately. In her stead was a red-brown wolf, her fangs bared and ready to strike.

And strike she did—lunging for my throat the first chance she got. Darkness flooded my vision again, but this time I could see just fine. The world was colored a dark blue as if someone had put colored lenses over my eyes. But more, it was like someone else was taking over, moving my body like a puppet. My legs tensed, springing from the ground *fast, fast, fast* as my body twisted. The hand with the blade in it snapped out, slashing in an upward stroke.

When my feet hit the floor, the wolf wasn't a wolf anymore. In the time it took me to land my jump, she'd phased back, clutching the side of her cheek where the blade had met her skin.

Her hand came away coated in red, her fingers shaking as she stared at them.

"Do you yield?" I felt myself say, my voice deeper, stronger.

Gemma's green irises flashed, and she pounced again, her bloody hands growing claws before my very eyes. Those claws reached for me, slashing like my blade had, only I wasn't there anymore. Without me telling them to, my feet moved me three feet to the side, and my hand snapped out again, the blackened blade slicing through the air.

This time when it made contact, the skin of her back opened, the wound weeping blood as she staggered to the ground.

"Do you yield?" my voice asked again, but it didn't sound like me anymore.

Tears filled Gemma's eyes, the rage seeming more for her helplessness than for the fact that she was actively attempting to kill her brothers.

She staggered to her knees, hate filling her eyes. But Gemma was full of hate already, hate for people she didn't know and couldn't understand, hate for things out of her control and refusing to benefit her. My feet took me closer to her, my legs bending so I could look her in the eye. My blade fit itself under her chin, the point pressing up into her flesh until she raised her jaw.

"Do. You. Yield?"

Gemma pulled her chin up and away from my blade, her eyes downcast. She nodded, but I wanted the words.

"Do you know what you have done? What you have stolen?"

She flicked her eyes up to mine while her body crouched lower. "I did what was necessary."

At her hiss, my head nodded and the hand that was empty, clapped itself to her head. "Since you don't understand, I'll show you."

When I'd decided to come here, I did the thing I most feared: I absorbed the souls of the victims, taking them inside myself so they could be taken to their rest. Except Simone. She could walk the earth until Sloane decided to claim her for Tartarus. But with their souls came the power, the energy, the understanding of just how painful their deaths had been.

Just how horrible Gemma was—how much hate she had in her.

As soon as my hand made contact, the memory of Lucy's death came to the forefront of my mind, and I shoved it into her head. How Gemma had bit into her neck, breaking her spine but not taking her life. How she was powerless, afraid, unable to move as she watched the other witches get slaughtered. As she tried to scream for help as the fire moved closer and closer, eventually reaching her.

Burning her alive.

By the time she experienced the full weight of Lucy's death, Gemma was screaming, batting away imaginary flames as her eyes rolled back in her head. Then she was quiet, her body falling to the stone floor like a sack of flour. She started seizing, her body flopping wildly as the memories flooded her. Then the fog of darkness lifted, the control I'd thought I'd lost returning. I stowed my blade in the sheath at my ankle, and stood, turning my back to the wolf and collected my affects from Bishop.

Holstering my guns and donning my jacket, I watched as Gemma continued to writhe on the ground, once again taking my seat. Sniffing, I checked my nails as I waited for Gemma to get it together. I supposed I should feel at least some pity, but at her utter lack of remorse, I just couldn't muster it.

"What did you do to her?" Cassius breathed, staring at the woman on the ground in horror.

I shifted my gaze from my nails to the alpha. "I let her experience the life she took, a nice lady who was in the wrong place at the wrong time. Gemma just got to feel every horror, every fear, every flicker of flame that burned Lucy Kirkland alive. And when she wakes up,

I'm going to show her Margo Hollins' death, and then Julia Simmons, Yana Michaels, and Felicia Loveless'. Because before you take her head—which I have no doubt you'll do—she needs to understand what she's done."

What's funny was, I would have shown Gemma mercy had her actions been an accident.

"She meant to kill those women. She stalked them, ripped out their throats, and set them on fire. Then she convinced her own flesh and blood that the lives they took meant nothing. That they were bad people who deserved it. Now, I'm all for justifiable homicide. I've taken my fair share of lives in battle—people who'd stolen lives, people who'd attacked me and mine—but these witches were harmless. They didn't have any power, any abilities. Green witches, kitchen witches, ones that worked in cards or candles. Not ones with an ounce of elemental or chaos magic. Not a single one of them could have defended themselves in battle."

Cassius sat back in his chair, assessing me. "You know this? For certain?"

"I do." I nodded. "I got to live it, so now Gemma gets to."

Her mother stepped forward, weaving through the crowd. "Stop this, my King. No one should have to experience—"

"Burning alive? I agree, and yet your children did it to someone not even a handful of hours ago, and the day before, they killed three men the same way, so I don't care what you think of me. I'm not the one who murdered innocents."

I saw the flicker of her action a second before her claws came out. Gemma's mother raced for me, fangs growing in her mouth as her talons reached for me. My boot found a home in her gut as I pushed her away, but her claws raked through the fabric of my jeans, slicing through the meat of my thigh. Blood poured from the four claw marks, staining my ripped jeans red.

Before I ever told my arm to move, a blade was in my hand and then it wasn't. The weight of the knife flew from my fingers almost as soon as it touched them, the sharpness of the blade twirling end over end as it sailed through the air. It landed with a sickening *thunk* in the center of the woman's neck.

Her fingers scrabbled at it much like my father had when he died, the visage of him knowing he was going to die seemed to superimpose itself over Gemma's mother. The same shock, the same knowledge, the same fear—all of it was there in her expression, and there was nothing I could do about it. My wound was already healed, hers would take her life.

Her sons screamed for her, and a part of me wished I

could take it back. Wished I could turn back time and not throw that knife. Wished I would have done this another way.

Cassius nodded his head, the sorrow at losing a pack member stark on his face, and I clenched my teeth so I wouldn't start bawling. I could undo this. I could if I just leant her a little bit of the energy the souls had given me. Without another thought, I dove for Gemma's mother, ripping the blade from her neck.

Then I gave.

Because I couldn't watch another parent die like mine had. I didn't care that she attacked me. I didn't care that her sons and daughter were trash. She needed to live. She gurgled for a moment, the blood spewing from the wound at her neck until the healing hit her. Her eyes met mine, and I could see the disappointment in them.

She hadn't wanted to live. She'd wanted to die with her daughter. It was the only reason she'd attacked. It was a desire I didn't understand and yet did all at the same time. Because when Dad died, I'd wanted to follow him, too.

When the wound closed completely, I grabbed her by the collar and pulled her to standing with me. "I am not a means to kill yourself. You have sons that actually need you. Think about them the next time you consider offing yourself for the sake of your own self-pity."

But I would end her daughter's suffering. At least for now.

Passing the mother off to an incredibly tall man with flaming red hair and a beard grown to his chest, I then reached down to Gemma and pulled the memory of Lucy's death back. I had no doubt she'd still remember the pain and anguish she'd caused, but at least the seizing should stop.

My gaze shifted to the alpha as I stood. "You'll spare the boys?"

Cassius nodded. "I will."

"Good. Agent Kenzari will take them into custody. And Gemma?"

Cassius' gaze drifted to the floor, staring in disgust at the unconscious woman at our feet. "She will be dealt with. She won't make it out of this room alive."

"And I can have your word on that?"

"Are you calling me a liar?"

This coming from the man who'd asked if the ghosts and my testimony could be trusted. "Haven't you already called me one? Twice?" I didn't particularly want to get into a wolfy pissing match, but I would if it meant I knew Gemma was going to be taken care of. "All I asked for was your word. If you can't give it to me, I'd rather put a bullet in her brain and save us all the trouble."

You're supposed to be playing nice, Adler.

I took a deep breath. "But I was under the impression your customs dictated another method of execution. All I need is your word as an alpha that Gemma will not live past today, and I will gladly leave you to your death rites."

Cassius bowed his head, but the revulsion on his face made his next words moot. "You have my word."

I waited for him to finish, but he didn't. Had Yazzie not given me such a thorough rundown of wolf customs, I probably would have nodded and smiled and left. But he had been very particular about words of binding, and how if made in front of the whole pack, it could not be broken, or his leadership would be forfeit.

"Your word for *what*? The whole thing or it's not binding. You and I both know that."

But the alpha did not continue. "You were going to let her go—shun her maybe—even though she killed ten people. Had she won against me, you would have let her kill me, is that right? With an ABI agent outside, one as witness, a death mage ready to fight, and your son—my father's best friend—in the room?"

The truth of it all was stamped on Cassius' face. I'd been so wrong about him, and it almost hurt that Dave's father was nothing like his son. Shifting my gaze to Uncle Dave, I saw the truth in his eyes as well. He didn't trust the alpha, and there was a damn good reason he was an Omega. Why he'd chosen a life alone rather than live with the pack.

The realization that not only were the wolves not our friends, but absolutely could not be trusted hit me square in the face.

Nodding, I pulled my gun and chambered a round.

"So be it."

19

I never thought this was where I'd be on my first day on the job.

Well, no one expects to be in the middle of a werewolf den at three in the morning. That's just crazy.

No, what I hadn't anticipated was that I'd be about to shoot my way out of said den or that performing a public execution was actually more beneficial to my health than what was about to go down.

"Sarina," I called to the lone ABI agent. "Is there an ABI or arcane version of Miranda Rights?" If I was going to do the nice thing and arrest everyone, I wanted to make sure it fucking well stuck.

The oracle snorted. "Nope. It's more of a 'get cuffed and pray you don't get shot' kind of thing, and less a 'get out on a technicality because the law sucks' thing. It's a definite step up from the way you're used to."

Considering I'd been arrested and served nine months in arcane prison for bullshit, I had to disagree, but I sure as hell wouldn't be doing it here. "Super. Can you and Dave cuff the boys for me and start taking them out?"

In answer, I got a pair of ratcheting sounds of cuffs being deployed, so I took that as a yes. I pulled my cuffs from their pocket on my belt and tossed them to Bishop. He snagged them in the air and began cuffing Gemma before I ever said a word, which was good because the air in the room was three steps past tense.

"This was unnecessary," I murmured, unable to keep the hurt out of my voice. "All of it. The deaths, the deal, your inaction. You could have told me the truth."

Cassius' face seemed carved out of marble, his silence speaking volumes. I shifted my gaze to Gemma's mother. "I doubt you'll appreciate this, but I'll put in a good word for your sons. I don't think they knew what she was doing."

Considering the woman tried to go the "suicide by cop" route, I doubted it, but it needed to be said.

Returning my eyes to the alpha, I inclined my head ever so slightly. He did not deserve my grace or deference, and I refused to give him either. "I will also inform the vampire queen that the culprits have been apprehended. Though, if there are any more fires, I'll know where to start looking."

Then I turned my back on Cassius, his pack, and Gemma's mother, the slight to their power probably not in my best interest, but at the moment, I really didn't give a fuck. Bishop did the same, hauling the unconscious wolf over his shoulder and walking out.

"There will be judgment," Cassius growled, his animal close to the surface if his voice was anything to go by.

I shot him a look over my shoulder. "Yes. There will be."

Before he could reply, I faced front and strode out of the house as if I didn't have a whole pack right behind me ready to pounce at any second. I didn't breathe my first sigh of relief until the gate came into view, but that was short-lived.

The quartet of wolves at the gate snarled in unison, blocking Sarina, Dave, and their perps from leaving. I was the only one not holding a perp, so I did the only thing I could—I let the power of those souls, the essence of the lives lost leak from my body.

Only…

Only it wasn't the bright lights and floating off the ground and the heat that made it seem like my flesh might be melting off. It was cold and dark, a silvery mist of power that seemed to come from Death himself.

Was this what Azrael had gifted me with that kiss to my forehead? This darkness?

"You have three seconds to open this gate, or I'm going to stop being nice, and I've been real fucking nice up until now."

The voice that came from my throat didn't sound like my own. It was darker, deeper, more masculine, but it seemed to do the trick. All four wolves had their tails between their legs as the gate opened wide.

The headlights of my Jeep were a welcome sight—as was the faint outline of Dave's Haunted Peak Police Department SUV. But I wondered what we were going to do with three perps and seating for two.

"Sleeping potion and a trunk, duh," Sarina said as Yazzie emerged from my Jeep.

He appeared rather surprised to see us all walking out of the gate. "Holy shit. You made it. I could have sworn I was going to have to report you DOA on your first day."

I shifted my head from side to side, popping my neck but not answering him. He didn't know just how close that had been to coming true.

"Is that blood I smell?" Yazzie asked, his dark eyes widening when he got a good look at my ripped, bloodstained jeans and the still-bleeding unconscious wolf on Bishop's shoulder.

"Yep," Bishop and I said at once. Bishop turned to me. "Where do you want her?"

Thinking about it for a few seconds, I said, "Dave's SUV. It's reinforced some, and I have no plans to wait for an ABI pickup. Yazzie should go with Dave and turn them in. Sleeping potions all around?"

Sarina let out a low chuckle. "Absolutely."

Dave unlocked his car and opened the back hatch. Bishop dumped Gemma in the back, and Sarina pulled a weird-looking gun from a spine holster, pumping three rounds into her before I realized they were sleeping potion ampules.

Sarina turned to Bran who was sniffling and shaking like a leaf. "See. She's just sleeping. See her breathing?"

He nodded his head. The twelve-year-old boy was nearly a head taller than the agent, but he didn't give her any trouble. "Do you know what's going to happen to us?"

Pity crossed her expression before she masked it. "Yes."

"Is Gemma going to die?"

Sarina didn't answer. Instead, she asked, "If those witches would have killed wolves, what would've happened?"

A realization dawned on Bran's face. "War," he breathed. "It would've started a war."

"Would those witches have survived the retribution? Would they have deserved to?"

Bran shook his head. "Are we going to die?"

Sarina's gaze softened. "Someday. But not today. Now, quit asking questions, and when you wake up, ask for a lawyer, okay, kid?"

She helped the cuffed kid into the back of the SUV, and Dave followed with his quarry.

Reynard eyed his captor, stopping just before he sat on the bench seat. "You really left the pack? Made a home for yourself on your own?"

Dave inclined his head. "I did. Can't say it was easy, not having one, but it was a better choice for me. The way things go sometimes, the politics—I was never going to make it in a pack like that."

Reynard's face fell. "He can't control them like he used to. He'll lose Alpha soon enough. Maybe…"

"Sorry, kid," Dave muttered, shaking his head. "Just because I'm his son, doesn't mean I'd be the next alpha. Ya'll frown on mixed breeds, and I'm not a Leblanc."

The boy nodded and folded himself into the SUV. Sarina snaked around Dave and pumped three rounds each into the boys, the silvery potion exploding against their chests and instantly putting them to sleep.

"You have an hour to get them to HQ. There isn't any traffic on 11 but 40 is a mess. You'll need to hoof it. Yazzie, go with him. Make sure the boss knows Adler collared them all in less than a day, will you?"

Yazzie hesitated. "You want me to ride with four wolves?"

Uncle Dave chuckled as he slammed the back door shut. "Will our wolf stench affect your delicate sensibilities? I thought you bears were made of sterner stuff."

Yazzie narrowed his eyes at Dave, but I answered for him.

"I want you to ride with three sleeping wolves and the closest man to a father I have left, you wimpy dickweed. Now, get in the fucking truck and quit being a liability. Jesus."

I mean, come the fuck on. It was way too early—or late—for this and stalling wasn't going to get them to the ABI any faster.

Yazzie's face buttoned all the way up. In fact, if his lips got any more pressed together, he'd be forced to eat through his nostrils for crying out loud. "Fine."

"That's the spirit, Jensen. Good teamwork." Yes, I was laying the sarcasm on pretty thick at that point, but I wasn't the one bitching out, now, was I?

Before Dave slid into the driver's seat, he wrapped an

arm around my shoulders and yanked me in for a hug. "I'm sorry for what I did in there," he whispered, pressing his cheek against the top of my head. "I acted like a dumb wolf, and I'm sorry. It won't happen again."

Chuckling, I replied, "Well, I'm not sorry for putting you on your ass, but I accept your apology. You were trying to protect me, so I know your heart was in the right place—even if you are a dumb wolf."

Uncle Dave gave me a squeeze and let me go, sliding into his rig and starting it up. I smacked the roof in farewell, and he sped off, getting on the road before those sleeping potions wore off.

"I really need to get the recipe Dahlia has," Sarina said, picking up on my thoughts. "Hers last until the subject is hit with a counter agent. I wonder if we can synthesize it for rounds."

The urge to scold her about reading thoughts seemed moot after I spent a few days unwillingly reading the thoughts of the people around me. Instead, I opened my arms and enveloped the small agent in a hug.

As soon as she settled into my arms, though, she immediately pulled back. "What the fuck, Darby?"

Confused, I took a generous step back. "What the fuck, what?"

She turned to Bishop, wide-eyed. "What the fuck? You left some shit out, my friend. A lot of shit. I'm going to get a nosebleed from all the info I just got, and that's not even the half of it."

Sarina snatched up my wrist and hauled me bodily to my Jeep. "Where are your keys," she demanded, not bothering to answer any questions or elaborate at all. "Never mind. They're in the damn ignition. This mess has me asking stupid questions already."

Dumbfounded, I let myself get dragged while Bishop asked the question I myself wanted to ask.

"What do you see?"

Sarina shook her head in a ticking sort of way, like she was searching for the right answer.

"Darkness. A lot of it. Bishop better drive. We need to go to that grave I keep seeing. Where is it?" She muttered that last bit to herself, like she was asking the universe to guide her in the right path.

A grave she keeps seeing... She couldn't mean...

"I don't—"

"Haunted Peak Memorial Cemetery," Bishop growled, his feet stalling on the road toward my Jeep. "Is that it?"

A coldness swallowed me up, the same dreadful frost that filled my belly when I'd woken up on that damn grave. I pulled my wrist from her grip, shaking my head as I backed up.

"I don't want to go there."

I couldn't put my finger on it, but I wasn't supposed to be at that cemetery. There was something wrong, something bad about that place. I shouldn't have woken up on that grave. I shouldn't have been there at all. There was a reason the whole town avoided it.

"You have to," Sarina insisted.

And so, we went.

20

Haunted Peak Memorial Cemetery hadn't always given me the creeps. All it had really taken was waking up on a grave exactly once, and well, all that safety from the lack of ghosts had been shot to shit.

Reluctantly, I followed Sarina and Bishop over the rather pitiful chain with the rusted-out sign that claimed the graveyard was closed. Weeks ago, Azrael had come to me in this cemetery disguised as a raven. When that raven had turned into a man, I could have sworn I was hallucinating. Sometimes, I still wonder if I had been.

If all of this since had been a dream. If I'd really died that night at the gorge with that silly poltergeist. I sometimes thought that it might have been better for everyone if I had.

Dad would be alive. Maybe Azrael would be, too. Sloane would be home.

But had I passed in that tiny stream, Essex would still be running around. I couldn't decide if it had all been worth it or not.

I also couldn't decide whether or not I wanted to move any closer to the headstone where I'd woken up.

"How much darkness are we talking about? Like a little, or a lot?" I hedged, trying to see if I could run to my Jeep in the time it took Bishop to shade jump to me.

Bishop caught my hand before I could sprint away, reeling me into his arms and wrapping me up in them. It was slightly comforting, but more, it was restraining, which I did not like until he dropped a blistering kiss to my lips.

Our tongues tangled in a way that made me want to jump his bones in the middle of this cemetery without so much as a fuck given to the potential witnesses. Then I started laughing in the middle of the kiss.

Jump his bones. In the middle of a cemetery. Bones.

"I feel like I'm missing the joke, babe," he murmured against the skin of my neck.

My giggles petered out enough for me to explain. "I wanted to jump your bones."

The lascivious grin he gave me said he really liked the idea, and I sort of forgot the joke for a second.

"Jesus fucking Christ," Sarina growled. "Really? You two can't keep it in your pants?" She stomped over to us, grabbed my wrist and yanked, pulling me toward the row of cracked and worn graves. "Which one is it?"

My feet unerringly took me to the illegible headstone, its dates buried under the wear of time—not that I would have been able to read them this far away, even if they weren't hidden under centuries of grime. "This is where Azrael appeared to me the first time."

Sarina sidled up next to me, and Bishop on the other side. His fingers twined in mine.

"Is this where you woke up?" he asked, squeezing my hand reassuringly.

I nodded, unable to voice the sheer terror at waking up where I most definitely should not be without so much as an inkling of how I'd gotten there. Moving forward, I let go of Bishop's hand and walked closer to the headstone. I'd gotten close enough to touch it, and for some reason, I had a visceral need to reach my hand into the dirt and start digging.

Then my ghostly grandfather decided to make an appearance, his nearly see-through body forming right in front of me. "I wouldn't do that, lass," he announced, scaring me so bad I nearly fell on my ass. "Go back where ya came from and don't come back to this place. Do ya hear me?"

"Jesus, fuck, Hildy. Warn a girl, will you? And where the fuck have you been? You said you were going to follow the witches, bu—"

Hildy's face made me stop my bitching. Well, that and the slicing motion he made to his throat. "Get out of here, lass. Now. Don't walk. Run. Do ya hear me?"

I was an obstinate person by nature, but when Hildy told me to run, I fucking well ran. Pivoting on a heel, I double-timed it to Bishop and Sarina, and grabbed their hands, yanking them with me without so much as a nod toward an explanation.

Unfortunately, Hildy's warning came a little too late.

A fireball sailed past my face in the tiny space in between Sarina's body and mine. The heat and hiss had me ducking my head, but my feet kept moving.

Well, until they didn't...

As if my body had a mind of its own—and namely, not mine—it halted, my hands dropped Sarina and Bishop's, and my feet pivoted to face the onslaught. The smart thing would have been to search for cover before I did that, but I no longer had control. Silvery mist coated my hands and arms, growing larger by the second as if fanned out around me.

Two witches stood across from me: one a lime-haired Stevie Nicks lookalike and the other a mousey brunette.

The same two witches who had blown up my fucking house.

The same two witches who were supposed to be in ABI custody right about then.

"Naughty witches," I said, but it wasn't me saying it at all. It wasn't my voice, even though it came from my throat, my mouth working all on its own. "You think you can keep me down there? You think you can stop me?"

Dread filled me as the mist grew. I wasn't in charge of my body. I wasn't in control of my power or my limbs. And that power I'd thought had come from Azrael?

Well, I had a sinking feeling this was *not* from him.

Not. At. All.

The green-haired witch's face cracked a slight grin as a cold sort of power covered her hands and frosted the ground around her. "I think I can, Aemon, and I don't give a shit what skin you're riding—even if it is a demigod. I'll take you down."

"I should have let her kill you like she wanted," my mouth said, "then I wouldn't have to deal with two frail witches who couldn't take me if they tried."

"You know," the brunette said, "when Davenport had us go undercover for this job, I figured it was a 'kill two birds with one stone' kind of thing. We'd get to 'accidentally' kill the skin you're riding, and we'd get to put the illustrious demon, 'Aemon,' down for good. Win-win. But you aren't going to go without a fight, are you?"

They'd played dumb so convincingly, I'd practically handed them to the ABI. I'd been fooled. Again. And now I had a demon inside me? How?

"Of course I won't go without a fight," Aemon said from my lips. "I like it topside—not stuck in that box." My hand gestured in the direction of the grave I'd woken up on.

"Darby?" Bishop said, and my head turned, a crooked smile on my mouth as my eyes assessed the man I loved.

"Sorry, lover boy, Darby's not here right now. Try back later, mm-kay?" My hand flicked the end of my ponytail. "Maybe show me the moves you put on this body. It's all she can think about, you know. I missed most of the show last time. Too many souls in there, not enough room." My shoulders shrugged. "I'm dying for a repeat."

If I was in control of my body right now, I would throw up.

As it was, I kind of just wanted to die a little bit, or maybe shove this thing inside me out.

A ball of flame hit me square in the chest while my head was turned, singeing my T-shirt for a second before the mist covering my arms put it out. The skin underneath was already blistered and weeping, but that was gone in an instant, healing as if it were never there.

Looking down, my fingers brushed the ashes off the fabric before my gaze locked on the green-haired witch. "That was rude. And here I thought we could be friends."

The mist on my arms curled like writhing snakes, growing bigger, wider, shoving through the air and twisting on the ground toward the witches. A slew of pops rent the air as about a dozen stinging hits landed against my back.

My gaze found Sarina, the gun full of sleeping potion still in her hand.

"Oh, how sweet. The little fortune teller decided to jump in the fray. Sorry, sweetheart, sleeping potions don't work on demons."

My arm struck out, the sweeping mist knocking into Sarina like it was a solid thing. She flew backward, sailing through the air to land in a heap on the thick grass.

The ball of black and purple magic that hit next really smarted as it collided against my chest where the fireball had just struck. My mouth lifted in a sort of half-grin as my eyes met Bishop's.

"Fight, Darby. Kick him out of you. You can—"

My arm waved again, only the magic didn't just

knock into Bishop—it crashed over him like a wave, slamming him onto the ground before picking him up and doing it all over again.

"No can do, lover boy. You can thank her daddy for that one. He healed her all right, but he also sealed her in her mind. I can't get in, but she can't get out. Sorry," Aemon said, shrugging my shoulders like it was no big deal.

Then my feet moved me *fast, fast, fast* like I had at the pack house, the sick mist of power racing ahead of me as it struck the witches. Sarina and Bishop got hit, sure, but what Aemon was doing with my power was something else.

It crashed into them like a hammer, pummeling them until they were nothing but bloody stains on the grass. The green-haired witch reached for my hand, the faint trace of flames coating her fingers before it, too, flickered and died. Her hand fell to the ground, the life leaving her in an instant.

The brunette witch was still hanging on, though— her breathing was ragged as she gripped the tufts of grass and attempted to crawl away. Her power leaking from her, the ground froze each place she touched.

My hands reached for her, my fingers nearly making contact before a wave of green magic knocked into me. Losing my footing, I fell to my ass as the power seized my limbs. In the next second, Hildy crunched across the semi-frozen ground toward me, top hat on his head, skull cane in his hand, and unearthly magic surrounding him in an undulating ball of light.

No, Hildy. He's too strong. He'll hurt you. Kill you.

But I couldn't say it, not with Aemon in charge of my mouth. I shoved, trying to get out of my mind, trying to take back control of my body, but the demon had been telling the truth. I was locked in here, unable to do anything but watch.

"Ya think ya can possess my granddaughter and get away with it?" Another tsunami of fiery green shoved me down, crushing me against the grass. "I don't bleedin' think so."

The laugh that came out of my damaged lungs sounded unhinged. "Oh, I think I can."

Another wave struck me, only this time, it didn't let up, the weight of Hildy's magic cutting off air, cutting off my breath. My heartbeat slowed to a crawl as I slowly suffocated. Spots filled my vision as the world tunneled.

"You think killing her will do the trick?" Aemon wheezed. "Like there aren't plenty of perfectly healthy people in the world. I'll take one of them, and on and on forever. You can't kill them all."

An orb of black and purple magic sailed through the air, only it didn't strike my body. No, it hit Hildy square in the chest, knocking him back enough that his magic sputtered and died. As soon as it lifted, Aemon sucked breath into my lungs, the tunnel lifting ever so slightly.

"No, O'Shea," Bishop growled, staggering toward us. His nose was bloody and one of his arms hung listlessly at his side. His legs appeared to be about a millisecond from collapsing from underneath him. "Stop."

"What're ya doing, boy? I almost had him," Hildy snarled, the green of his magic growing from his body like a physical thing ready to crash into me at any moment.

"Did you?" Aemon growled from my throat, and my arm shot out, the silvery misting power slamming into Hildy's solid body like an anvil.

Then Hildy wasn't solid anymore, his ghostly gray form became incorporeal in an instant, but still he was down, struggling to stand after the onslaught.

"Looks like all you did was piss me off, grave talker." My arms yanked the power back and shoved my body up from the ground, my legs staggering toward the grave. I pivoted, swinging back to stare at Bishop.

"Raise me, mage. Raise me and I'll free your woman."

Bishop's knees gave out, and he knelt on the grass. "No."

My head tilted. "No? I think you will. In fact, I'd be

willing to bet her life on it—much like her grandfather was going to do."

Then things got *really* weird.

A ripping sensation ricocheted through my rib cage, and I watched in horror as what I could only describe as a soul rise from my chest. See-through and yet solid, the form seemed to take the shape of a man's torso, his visage pretty but wrong all at the same time.

But as soon as he peeled himself from my body, the breath in my lungs stalled, my heart—which had been tripping double-time—stuttered and stopped. My legs collapsed underneath me, my knees hitting the grave hard enough to bruise. I wanted to move, shove Aemon the rest of the way out, but I was still powerless, still unable to do anything but watch.

"She's dying, you know," the demon said, his tone so blasé about the fact that he was killing me. The fact that he was still using my voice to do it was icing on the cake. "I figure you have another minute or two before brain damage sets in from oxygen deprivation, but do take your time."

"If she dies—"

"I'll just hijack another body. No one wards like they should anymore. Even that little ABI witch trying to crawl away is ripe for the picking." Aemon tutted a bit, the disappointment in his voice completely and utterly fake.

Don't do it. Don't give him what he wants. Please. If you love me at all, don't do it.

But Bishop couldn't hear me. No one could.

"You will let her go if I do this—raise your grave?" Bishop growled through gritted teeth. "Alive and unharmed?"

"I give you my word as a demon. Darby Adler will be alive and whole, healed and protected from further possession."

I saw the moment Bishop decided to agree—the exact second that he chose me over the rest of the world.

"I accept."

Well, fuck.

21

It was a very strange thing to know that the man you loved, loved you more than anyone or anything on the planet. I mean, why else would he decide setting a demon free to walk the earth was a stellar plan? In the realm of ultimatums, killing me was a good one, but a demon?

Really?

Bishop staggered to standing. "Let her breathe. Please. I'll do it, just…"

"Oh, fine," Aemon muttered. "If it'll get you to get the lead out. I've been trapped in that damn coffin for centuries. Stalling is very high on the list of actions that will negate our little deal—no matter how much I want—"

"Don't," Bishop barked, cutting him off.

"Disrespecting her and her body is not acceptable. It's bad enough you're using her like a puppet."

Aemon retracted into my body, allowing me to suck in a huge breath. The spots once again left my vision as my heart's rhythm got back on track. "If it really offends you so, I'll stop. Just please. The box. I would like to get out of it."

Gold tinted Bishop's eyes as his jaw clenched, a faint tinge of rage coloring his face as black swirls crept up his arms. The ground beneath my feet shook, and Aemon staggered backward out of the way.

In a matter of seconds, an odd coffin-like box broke through the ground, rising like a piece of ice in a glass, the ground shunning it altogether. The buoyed box sat there, its blackened wood and blood-red sigils shining in the faint glow of the surrounding streetlights.

"Open it," Aemon ordered, his voice hungry.

Bishop shook his head, a sly smile on his lips. "That wasn't the deal. I rose your coffin. No one said anything about letting you out of that box."

Aemon's screech of rage filled the air as my body lunged, power snaking out of my hands and slamming into Bishop with the force of a wrecking ball. "Open that fucking box, mage. I know you can."

Blood coated Bishop's smile as he struggled to breathe, but he still said a resounding, "No."

*Please stop. Please. Please don't make me watch him die.
Please...*

"I'll kill her," Aemon warned, making my hands
wrench the man I loved from the ground and shake him.
"I'll—"

"You won't," Bishop gasped, his head flopping on his
neck. "You need her too much. She's your only
leverage."

Aemon dropped him to the ground, a frustrated
growl ripping up my throat. My feet stalked over to the
dying witch, the one still trying and failing to crawl
away. My hands ripped her from the ground and dragged
her bodily to the sigil-laden box.

"Open it."

The brunette gasped out a pathetic, "No," but failed
to enforce the gravitas that Bishop had.

My fingers tightened around her throat, squeezing
just hard enough that the threat of death was a very real
thing. "Open it. Now."

The witch nodded, her big brown eyes full of sorrow.
Then my fingers pulled a blade from my boot, showing it
to the small woman. "Your hand, witch."

Reluctantly, she offered it, and the blade came down,
slashing her palm wide open. Blood bloomed from her
flesh, and the witch slapped her palm on the box, letting
the blood flow into the center sigil.

A faint hiss sounded, but the box didn't open, and a frustrated growl erupted from my throat. In an instant, the blade slashed again, only this time, it hit the woman's jugular, spilling all her blood on the wood. The poor woman gasped once, twice, and then she wilted as my arms picked her up and let her dying lifeblood flow over the coffin.

No. Nononononononono…

The hiss was louder this time, the lid of the coffin popping up as if a lock was sprung. A smile stretched my mouth as the witch was tossed away from my body like trash. Aemon did not care that someone had lost their life.

My fingers fit into the small gap provided and jerked the lip up and open. A sleeping man lay in the pristine coffin, his face pretty and preserved and not like any demon I'd ever thought of. The next second, the ripping feeling in my chest was back as Aemon wrenched himself from me—flowing back into himself.

It took a second for my body to return to my control, so I laid there watching as a shiny loafer-clad foot emerged from the coffin. It was quickly followed by a second, both attached to black trouser-encased legs. A handsome—if entirely evil—face emerged in my eyeline, blue eyes dancing as a grin stretched his face wide.

"I appreciate the assist, love," Aemon said, his voice

smooth as silk and exactly what I'd figure a demon sounded like. "If you hadn't jumped through that portal Mariana rigged up, I'd still be moldering in that coffin. And just because I'm such a good guy, I'll keep my end of the deal your lover boy tried to weasel out of. I'll heal you, make you whole, and make sure no one else rides that sexy little body of yours."

He seemed rather disappointed at the idea. "Though, it is too bad. I'd love to make use of it again, but I have a feeling you wouldn't like it the second time around."

The first time hasn't exactly been a picnic, asshole.

Aemon giggled—honest-to-god giggled. "Oh, good. I can read your thoughts again. You are a cheeky little thing. I look forward to seeing you again."

Then the demon knelt at my side, brushing a single fingertip from my forehead to my nose, over my lips and down my throat. Once he reached the center of my chest, he stopped, pressed the pad of his finger into my flesh, and a smile once again bloomed on his face.

In the next instant, pain unlike I'd ever felt hit me. It was worse than the souls being ripped from me, worse than the burning, worse than anything. Every part of me, every nerve ending, every cell was made of pain, of torment. And then, like a crack of lightning, it was gone.

"There. All healed up. Though I did make you unable to get up for a few minutes. Got to give myself a head start and all that." He pinched the end of my nose, wiggling it like a grandma would a toddler. "Tootles, Darby. Can't wait to meet again."

And then Aemon was gone, winking out of sight as if this had all been a bad dream. Hell, if I wasn't still stuck, unable to move, I'd have believed it was.

The best I could do was breathe and blink, and even that took willpower and a hell of a lot of effort.

A demon is free, Darby. A demon is free to walk the fucking earth and you're worried about blinking? Seriously?

My inner bitch was spot on. There was a demon walking the earth, and it wasn't some inconsequential non-corporeal demon possessing a cemetery groundskeeper, either. This was someone bad enough to get locked up for centuries. He gave exactly zero fucks about taking lives to get what he wanted, too.

"Darby?" Bishop croaked. "Darby!"

But I couldn't answer him. Luckily, Sarina could.

"She's alive," she called, her voice faint it was so far away. "And all healed up. I'm not, though, so when you get yourself together, come get me. My goddamn leg is broken."

A wave of relief washed over me, and a lone tear crested my eyelid and fell freely down my cheek. All I needed was proof Hildy wasn't a dead ghost—was that even a thing?—and I could breathe easy.

A second later, his grayed-out, see-through head appeared above me.

"Ah, lass," he muttered, his face awash with regret and a bit of shame. "I'm sorry."

Hildy had tried to sacrifice me, true, but as someone who'd done plenty of that over the last year, well, I couldn't say I blamed him.

"I thought if you'd died a little bit, I could convince Sloane to make sure it didn't stick as it were, you know? Seemed a better plan than setting a Prince of Hell free."

I felt my eyes widen, and I was so stunned at the Prince of Hell shit, I couldn't even marvel at the fact that I could move my eyes a bit more.

Prince of Hell? Is he fucking serious?

Hildy nodded. "Yep, lass. We are well and truly fucked."

He wasn't lying.

"Wait, what?" J said, stunned, his big body plopping onto the couch of the Warden house. "On your first day on the job you managed to incite discord with the werewolf pack, solve ten murders, and raise a demon?" He shifted his gaze to Jimmy who sat next to him just as stunned. "Did I leave anything out?"

He may have skipped over the accidental murdering

of two ABI agents, but before I could allow the pain of that knowledge to take root, Sarina rolled up an issue of *Vogue* and slapped me upside the head with it.

Let me tell you, Vogue doesn't skimp on pages, so that shit hurt. A lot.

"Ow," I groaned. "What the fuck?"

Sarina narrowed her eyes at me. "Every time you mentally take the blame for anything that happened at that fucking cemetery, I'm doing it again. I might even employ a brick if need be."

"Okay. Jesus," I said, throwing my hands up. "No blame. Got it."

Anything to not get hit in the head, sure—even if I thought it was damn impossible to police my own thoughts.

"Agent Bancroft made a deal with a demon, and she got herself and her partner killed. That is what happened, got it?" Sarina's eyebrows made a home for themselves super close to her hairline, a sure sign that I had zero time to waste arguing or I'd get slapped with the magazine again.

"Got it."

She directed her attention to the three men sitting on the couch. "Got it?"

Jimmy and J nodded vigorously, but Bishop didn't. Instead, he met my gaze, shame in his.

"I fucked up," he breathed, pain clearly lacing each word. "I thought I could outwit him, but—"

"Stop it," I whispered. "You did everything you could. Hell, you were ready to die to keep him down. Sarina's right. Bancroft made the deal that freed him. Not you."

It was semantics, sure, but that was the story I was sticking to, dammit. "What I want to know is how Davenport knew I was possessed in the first place, and why he didn't just tell someone—fuck *anyone*—except two witches who seemed rather keen on killing me rather than getting the demon out? None of it makes any sense."

"It does if you know Davenport," a rough male voice muttered from behind me, and I turned to see Acker leaning against the doorframe.

Great. He'll tattle as soon as he gets a chance.

"That's just it. I don't know Davenport," I replied, my whole body tensing.

Acker gave me a derisive snort. "Obviously, or else you wouldn't have taken this job."

Shrugging, I said, "It was this or prison. Well, I think prison. The other option might have been death. Not much of a choice, really."

"Fair enough. Davenport wants on the council. Hates the fact that he has to answer to them. The only thing he hates more? You. You've been showing the ABI up for years with how you deal with the arcaners in this town. With this little bit of unrest?" Acker chuckled and shook his head. "He'll exploit it until the day you die. And setting a demon free? You'll catch the blame no matter what."

Super. Just what I need. More shit to worry about.

"Which totally explains this summons," he said, offering me a pressed linen envelope.

I swallowed. "Could you open it for me? Show it to me?"

"I'll get the evidence tongs." J sighed, shoving himself up from the couch.

Acker frowned at me, clearly confused.

"My brother spelled a note with a blood curse—had a proclivity for them. I damn near died. My sister actually did die—though, since she was technically already dead, it didn't stick. Notes with that kind of paper make me nervous."

Understanding dawned. "Gotcha. That makes sense."

"Really?" I sat back on my stool, surprised. "I thought I sounded like a lunatic."

Acker opened the note as he lifted a single beefy shoulder. "I specialize in this kind of magic. There are few of us in the world, and to have it used in such a way is..." His eyes widened when I got up from my seat and took a healthy step back. "Oh, no. I don't have magic—not that kind, anyway. I just study it. I can't hurt you."

"The hell you can't," Jimmy growled. "Why the fuck do they have a Mormo topside? I thought your kind was extinct." At my confused stare, Jimmy elaborated. "A Mormo feasts on the blood of children, though typically, they're female."

Acker's face fell. "I don't do that. Not since…"

Understanding dawned. *Not since he killed his twin.*

"I had my powers bound almost a century ago. Linus was… I don't even eat red meat anymore. I'm as safe as I can make myself. I study blood bonds because I don't know my parents, and I study curses, because one of these days, I'd like to lift the one on me. I can't hurt anyone—not by magic, anyway."

"I see," I murmured. "Want to open that note for me. Tell me if you see any blood magic woo-woo?"

Acker blinked at me, relief crossing his face before he broke the seal of the note open. "Your presence is requested…" He rattled off an address and something about an audience with the council. "…formal attire required, twelve a.m. sharp."

"Do they mean tonight?" I squawked.

Acker flipped the note over. "Looks like it."

The doorbell rang, and I startled like someone had zapped me with a cattle prod. Without much thought on my part, I raced for the door, snatching it open like it might give me some reprieve.

On the other side was a very well-dressed man with severe features and a head of silvery-black hair. A jagged scar ran through his left eye, leaving the iris a pale blue. The right eye was a rather pretty hazel, and both seemed to stare right through me.

"Ms. Adler, allow me to introduce myself," he said, his voice an ominous rasp. "I am Deimos. I believe you freed my son."

Oh. Shit.

Darby's story will continue with
Dead Ahead
Grave Talker Book Five

DEAD AHEAD

Grave Talker Book Five

Some secrets should stay buried.

After accidentally freeing a demon, ticking off the werewolf alpha, and possibly inciting a war, Darby Adler's Warden job is in serious peril.

With the council up in arms and a literal god on her doorstep, Darby needs to figure her life out and pronto.

If she can't, losing her job might be the least of her problems.

Preorder on Amazon today!
Coming February 22, 2022

Want to get to know Darby's sister? Check out…

NIGHT WATCH

Soul Reader Book One

Waking up at the foot of your own grave is no picnic… especially when you can't remember how you got there.

There are only two things Sloane knows for certain: how to kill bad guys, and that something awful turned her into a monster. With a price on her head and nowhere to run, choosing between a job and a bed or certain death sort of seems like a no-brainer.

If only there wasn't that silly rule about not killing people...

Grab Night Watch today!

SPELLS AND SLIP-UPS

The Wrong Witch Book One

I suck at witchcraft.

Coming from a long line of famous witches, I should be at the top of the heap. Problem is, if there is a spell cast anywhere in my vicinity, I will somehow mess it up.

As a probationary agent with the Arcane Bureau of Investigation, I have two choices: I can limp along and *maybe* pass myself off as a competent agent, or I can fail. *Miserably.*

Worse news? If I can't get my act together, I may not only be out of a job, I could also lose my life.

Whose idea was this again?

Preorder now!
Coming June 7, 2022

THE PHOENIX RISING SERIES

an adult paranormal romance series by Annie Anderson

Heaven, Hell, and everything in between. Fall into the realm of Phoenixes and Wraiths who guard the gates of the beyond. That is, if they can survive that long...

Living forever isn't all it's cracked up to be.

Check out the Phoenix Rising Series today!

EXCLUSIVE SNEAK PEEKS,
GIVEAWAYS, BOOK DISCUSSION.
COME FOR THE BOOKS.
STAY FOR THE MEMES.

To stay up to date on all things Annie Anderson, get exclusive access to ARCs and giveaways, and be a member of a fun, positive, drama-free space, join The Legion!

ABOUT THE AUTHOR

Annie Anderson is the author of the international bestselling Rogue Ethereal series. A United States Air Force veteran, Annie pens fast-paced Urban Fantasy novels filled with strong, snarky heroines and a boatload of magic. When she takes a break from writing, she can be found binge-watching The Magicians, flirting with her husband, wrangling children, or bribing her cantankerous dogs to go on a walk.

To find out more about Annie and her books, visit www.annieande.com